THE ILLUSTRATED

CHARLES DICKENS

Adapted by
Nigel Flynn and Richard Widdows

This edition published 1993 in the United Kingdom by MMB,
an imprint of Multimedia Books Limited,
32 - 34 Gordon House Road, London NW5 1LP

Editors: Nigel Flynn and Richard Widdows
Design: Janette Place
Jacket design: Peter Bennett
Production: Hugh Allan

A catalogue record for this book is available
from The British Library

ISBN 1-85375-130-8

Printed in the Czech Republic by Imago

CONTENTS

The Life of Charles Dickens

Charles John Huffham Dickens was born on 7 February 1812, in the English coastal town of Portsmouth, where his father, John Dickens, was a clerk in the Navy Pay Office. John Dickens was 26 when Charles was born and was an excitable, extravagant man who liked to entertain in style — a style that his meagre salary as a clerk was unable to support. This was to lead him into a succession of financial crises throughout his life.

The second of eight children, Charles was a delicate, sensitive child, unable to join in the play of other children, and he withdrew into books. Later in life, recalling his boyhood days, he wrote: "When I think of it, the picture always arises in my mind of a summer evening, the boys at play in the churchyard and I sitting on my bed, reading as if for life."

The books that he read, introduced to him by his father — books such as *Robinson Crusoe*, *The Arabian Nights*, *Don Quixote* and a child's *Tom Jones* — created for him a world of magic, wonder and adventure, a world that he himself was so vividly to create for others to enjoy in his own books.

At the age of 12 the childhood of Dickens came to a sudden and dramatic end. His father, unable to pay his large debts, was packed off to the Marshalsea Debtors' Prison in London. Within a few days the rest of the family were to join him there — all, that is, except Charles, whose education was cut short and who was made to earn his living, washing bottles, at Warren's Blacking Factory. This experience proved so shocking and humiliating to the boy that it was to haunt him for the rest of his life. "No words can express the secret agony of my soul . . . I felt my early hopes of growing up to be a learned and distinguished man crushed in my breast."

Though soon re-united with his family, the previous easy life enjoyed by Charles was never to return. Two years later, at the age of 14, his irregular and inadequate schooling ended and he began work as a clerk in a lawyer's office in Gray's Inn, London. This experience, again not a happy one, gave him two things — a lifelong loathing of the legal profession and much raw material for many of his later novels.

Dickens then became a reporter on the parliamentary newspaper *True Sun*, where his natural talent for reporting and keen observation was first recognized. He taught himself shorthand and, on the *Mirror of Parliament*, and then the *Morning Chronicle*, he was soon acknowledged as the best parliamentary reporter of the age.

In 1833, now very much the young man about town, Dickens wrote his first piece of fiction: *A Dinner at Poplar Walk*, in the *Old Monthly Magazine*. Asked by the editor to contribute more, under the pen name 'Boz', Dickens wrote a series of pieces that were collected and published in 1836 under the title *Sketches by Boz*.

The modest success of *Sketches* was followed by the enormously popular and successful *Pickwick Papers*, which was published in monthly instalments in 1836 and 1837. Pickwick became a national hero overnight, and his exploits were followed by an average of 40,000 readers. Though not yet 30, Dickens was now rich and famous.

Two days after the publication of Pickwick, Dickens married Catherine Hogarth, daughter of a fellow journalist. "So perfect a creature never breathed," he wrote of her at the time, "she had not a fault." But with time his view of her was to change, and in later years he was to admit, "She is amiable and complying but nothing on earth would make her understand me." They were to separate in 1858, when Dickens was 46.

Throughout his life Dickens enjoyed travelling. In the 1840s he journeyed to Scotland, America, France, Switzerland and Italy. And throughout this period he poured out a succession of novels that exposed the cruelty, hypocrisy and appalling poverty of early Victorian society, novels such as *Oliver Twist*, *Nicholas Nickleby*, *The Old Curiosity Shop*, *Barnaby Rudge*, *A Christmas Carol*, *Martin Chuzzlewit*, and *Dombey and Son*.

Even his novel writing (which continued to be published in monthly instalments) proved inadequate for his boundless energy and restless spirit. In the 1840s, apart from all his major novels, and work on *David Copperfield* (published in 1850), he started a daily newspaper, the *Daily News*, and a weekly magazine, *Household Words*, in addition to writing a travel book *American Notes* and a three-volume *Child's History of England*.

In all that he wrote Dickens strove to draw people together and lead them to a better understanding of each other. As he himself believed, "In this world a great deal of bitterness among us arises from an imperfect understanding of one another."

But as he grew older, the subjects he wrote of grew bleaker and the mood more grim. *Bleak House, Hard Times, Little Dorrit, A Tale of Two Cities, Great Expectations, Our Mutual Friend* and his unfinished novel, *The Mystery of Edwin Drood*, all reflect a growing pessimism.

Despite a steady decline in health, Dickens continued to give dramatic public readings of his works to packed houses in both Britain and the United States, which he visited again in 1867–68. Of these a contemporary witness reported, "He seemed to be physically transformed as he passed from one character to another; he had as many distinct voices as his books had characters; he held at command the fountains of laughter and tears . . . When he sat down it was not mere applause that followed, but a passionate outburst of love for the man."

But the strain proved too much and on 8 June 1870, during a farewell series of talks in England, he suffered a stroke, and the next day he died at his home, Gad's Hill Place, near Rochester, Kent, at the age of 58.

Two days after his death Queen Victoria wrote in her diary, "He is a very great loss. He had a large loving mind and the strongest sympathy with the poorer classes." On 14 June he was buried in Poet's Corner, Westminster Abbey, close to the monuments of Chaucer and Shakespeare.

Charles Dickens in his study at Gad's Hill Place, his home near Rochester, Kent, reproduced by kind permission of the Trustees of the Dickens House (*Dickens' Dream* by R. W. Buss)

Oliver Twist

Introduction

OLIVER TWIST is one of the most popular stories of all time, and it tells the story of a boy's journey from hell to heaven.

For children like Oliver, England a hundred and fifty years ago was a cruel, hard place. At his birth, Oliver's mother dies. Unloved and uncared for, he grows up in the workhouse, ill-treated and half-starved by the dreadful Mr Bumble, the beadle. When he asks for more food, he speaks for hundreds of thousands of children everywhere whose voices society refuses to hear.

Dickens had a deep desire to expose neglect and abuse and make the world a better place for the poor and weak, and in *Oliver Twist* he uses Mr Bumble and the fiendish Fagin to represent cruelty and tyranny. Fagin is one of Dickens' most evil characters; at one point Dickens refers to him as a "merry old gentleman", a nineteenth-century name for the Devil himself. Be cruel to children, Dickens says, and they will turn to a life of crime: when Oliver arrives in London the Artful Dodger befriends him and takes him straight to Fagin's den.

Oliver is plunged into a nightmare world from which he cannot escape; he tries to, but is hunted down and caught. When his only true friend, Nancy, tries to escape she is horribly murdered.

There are good people in *Oliver Twist* too, including Oliver. In his heart he is not coarsened by the workhouse or corrupted by Fagin. Like Christian in *The Pilgrim's Progress*, he finds peace and safety in the end, helped by Mr Brownlow, Dr Losberne, Rose Maylie and Nancy. In the end goodness wins over evil.

Oliver Twist was Dickens' second novel. After the fun and humour of *The Pickwick Papers*, it rather surprised his readers, but it sold well and added to his growing reputation. Today *Oliver Twist* is the most widely read of all his novels, and Dickens would have been pleased to know that a story which shows "the principle of Good surviving through every adverse circumstance" has remained so popular.

1 In the Workhouse

On a cold, wet night, in a workhouse in a certain town in England, on a day and a date which are unknown, a baby boy was born.

For a long time after he was ushered into this world it remained a matter of doubt whether he would survive. He had no one to help or comfort him but an old pauper nurse and his poor, young mother who lay dying in bed.

Feebly the young woman raised her pale face from the pillow and in a faint voice said, "Let me see my baby before I die."

"Lor bless her heart," said the old nurse. "When you has lived as long as I 'ave and had thirteen children and all on 'em dead 'cept two, and them in the workhouse with me, you'd know better than to take on in that way."

But the young woman just shook her head and stretched out her hand towards the child. She kissed the baby passionately on its forehead with her cold, white lips.

"Keep him safe," she whispered, "and when he's grown up, give him this . . ."

She pressed a gold locket into the old nurse's hand, then gazed wildly round, shuddered, fell back — and died.

"Poor dear," said the old nurse as she stooped to pick the baby up. "It's all over."

By the light of a flickering candle, the old nurse snatched the locket from the dead woman's hand. Opening it, she saw the name 'Agnes' engraved inside.

Then stuffing the locket into her pocket, she carried the crying child out of the room and up a shabby flight of stairs to Mr Bumble's office.

Mr Bumble was the beadle in charge of the workhouse, and on this night — as on most nights — he was entertaining his friends to drinks. They were laughing and joking when the old woman knocked on the door.

"Mr Bumble," she called out, "Mr Bumble!"

"And what do you want?" demanded Mr Bumble rudely as he opened the door.

"It's this baby, begging your pardon, sir."

"Oh, not another one! Well, what is it — boy or girl?"

"Please, sir, it's a boy."

"Name?"

"Sally, sir."

"No, not your name, you fool! The boy's name!"

"Don't know, sir. He 'ain't got no name."

"No name!" boomed Mr Bumble. "Why ever not? What's his mother call him?"

"Mother's dead, sir."

"How very inconsiderate of her! Well, I'll just have to invent a name for him myself."

Mr Bumble went to his desk and took out a notebook. "We name all our fondlins in alphabetical order. The last was an S — Swubble, I name him. So this one must be a T — Twist. Yes, I think I'll call him Twist. Oliver Twist."

"Queer sort of name, if you ask me," replied old Sally.

"Well, nobody did ask you. And you'd better get used to it, Sally. Master Oliver Twist is going to be on our hands for the next ten years!"

Oliver cried lustily. If he could have known that he was an orphan left to the tender mercies of Mr Bumble and the workhouse, perhaps he would have cried even louder.

Nine years passed with little improvement in the condition of the workhouse — or of Mr Bumble's temper. Oliver Twist's ninth birthday found him a pale, thin child somewhat lacking in height. But nature had implanted a good sturdy spirit in Oliver's breast. It had plenty of room to expand, thanks to the spare diet of the workhouse. And perhaps it was surprising that he had survived to celebrate his ninth birthday at all. Be this as it may, however, it *was* his ninth birthday and he was keeping it in the same way as he had all previous birthdays, or for that matter almost every day of his life.

The room in which Oliver and the other boys of the workhouse were fed was a large stone hall with a huge copper pot at one end. Out of this, the master, dressed in cook's uniform, and assisted by one or two women, ladled out gruel at meal-times. Of this delicious concoction each boy had one ladleful, and no more. The bowls never wanted washing. The boys polished them with their spoons till they shone, and when they had performed this operation — which never took very long, the spoons being nearly as large as the bowls — they would sit staring at the large

copper pot with such eager eyes as if they could have devoured it and the very table it was standing on.

For years Oliver Twist and his companions had suffered the tortures of slow starvation. At last they grew so voracious and wild with hunger, that one boy proposed that they should draw lots; whoever drew the shortest should walk up to the master after supper that night and ask for more.

The evening arrived; the boys took their places. The master stationed himself at the copper as usual, his assistants ranged behind him. The gruel was served out and a long grace was said. The gruel disappeared. The boys whispered and nudged each other. Anxiously they drew the lots. And the shortest fell to Oliver!

Young as he was, Oliver was desperate with hunger and reckless with misery. He rose from the table and advancing to the master, basin and spoon in hand, said in a thin, nervous voice, "Please, sir, I want some more."

The master was a red-faced man, but now he turned very pale. He gazed in stupefied astonishment at Oliver for several seconds and then clung to the copper for support.

"What!" he said at length, in a weak voice.

"Please, sir," replied Oliver, "I want some more."

"More! More?" he boomed and he aimed a blow at Oliver's head with the ladle, picked him up roughly by the scruff of his neck, and marched him out of the room shrieking, "Mr Bumble! Mr Bumble!"

The beadle was sitting with his friends when the master burst into his office shouting, "Mr Bumble, begging your pardon, sir, but Oliver Twist has asked for more!"

There was a general start. Horror was

depicted on every face.

"For *more?*" shouted Mr Bumble.

"He did, sir," replied the master.

"That boy will be hung," said a gentleman in a white waistcoat. "I know that boy will be hung."

No one disputed the prophetic gentleman's opinion. An animated discussion took place, and Oliver was ordered into instant confinement. Next morning, Mr Bumble posted a notice on the outside of the workhouse, offering a reward of five pounds to anyone who would take Oliver Twist off the hands of the parish.

"I never was more convinced of anything in my life," said the gentleman in the white waistcoat as he knocked at the gate and read the bill next morning: "I never was more convinced of anything in my life, than I am, that that boy will come to be hung."

2 Apprenticed to a Coffin-Maker

Early that same day Mr Bumble was returning to the workhouse when he encountered, at the gate, Mr Sowerberry the undertaker.

"I have measured up the two women that died last night, Mr Bumble," said the undertaker.

"You'll make your fortune, Mr Sowerberry," said the beadle as he thrust his thumb and forefinger into the coffin-shaped snuff-box offered him by Mr Sowerberry.

"Think so?" said the undertaker. "Well I have you to thank, Mr Bumble, seeing as how you provide me with more business than anyone else in the parish."

"By the bye," said Mr Bumble, "you don't know anybody who wants a boy, do you?" And as he spoke he raised his cane to the poster above him, and gave three distinct taps on the words, 'five pounds reward'.

"Well, I was just thinking, Mr Bumble, I could do with a boy myself. Someone to walk in front of the funeral procession, someone with a pale, sad face, to emphasize the misery, the dismal nature of the occasion."

"That's young Oliver exactly," replied Mr Bumble, grasping the undertaker by the arm and leading him into the building. Within minutes it was arranged that Oliver should go to Mr Sowerberry's that evening.

Oliver heard the news in perfect silence. And having had his luggage, which consisted of a small, brown paper parcel, put into his hand, he pulled his cap over his eyes and attaching himself to Mr Bumble's coat-cuff, was led away to a new scene of suffering.

Mr Sowerberry was making some entries into his day-book by the light of a dismal candle when Charlotte, the maid, showed Mr Bumble in.

"Mrs Sowerberry! Mrs Sowerberry!" cried the undertaker. "Come here a moment, my dear!"

"Dear me," said Mrs Sowerberry seeing Oliver, who gave a bow, "he's very small."

"He *is* small," replied Mr Bumble, "there's no denying it. But he'll grow, Mrs Sowerberry — he'll grow."

"I dare say he will, Mr Bumble, on our food and our drink. There! Get down stairs, little bag o' bones." And with this, the undertaker's wife opened a side-door and pushed Oliver down a steep flight of stairs to a lonely cell, damp and dark.

"Here, Oliver, you can have some of the cold bits that were put by for the dog. I dare say you ain't too dainty to eat 'em, are you, boy?"

"No indeed, thank you, ma'am," replied Oliver, whose eyes had glistened at the sight of meat and who was trembling with eagerness to devour it.

When Oliver had finished eating his supper, Mrs Sowerberry, taking up a dim and dirty lamp, led the way upstairs.

"You don't mind sleeping among the coffins, do you?" said Mrs Sowerberry. "Not that it

matters whether you do or don't! You can't sleep anywhere else!"

Left to himself, Oliver set the lamp down on a bench and gazed timidly about him with a feeling of awe and dread. Nor were these the only dismal feelings which depressed him. He was alone in a strange place. He had no friends to care for, or to care for him. And he wished, as he crept into his lonely bed that night, that it were *his* coffin; that he could be laid in a calm and lasting sleep in the churchyard, with tall grass waving gently above his head and the sound of church bells soothing him to sleep.

The next morning Oliver was awakened by a loud kicking at the outside of the shop door.

"Open the door, will yer?" cried a voice. "I suppose you're the new boy, ain't yer?" asked the voice again when Oliver had done as he had been told.

"Yes, sir."

"Yer don't know who I am, do yer, Work'us? Well I'm Mister Claypole and you take orders from me, right? Now take down those shutters, yer idle young ruffian!" And with this, Mr Claypole, who in reality was not much older or bigger than Oliver, gave Oliver a hearty kick.

So began for Oliver many months of ill-treatment at the hands of Noah Claypole, who abused him far worse when he learned that Oliver was to lead the funeral procession while he, Noah, was to remain in the shop.

Oliver had been in Mr Sowerberry's employment some three months when an event occurred that was to prove very important in his life.

Seated one dinner-hour in the kitchen, and feeling in a particularly vicious mood, Noah decided to tantalize and aggravate Oliver even more than usual.

" 'Ow's yer mother, Work'us?" he said.

"She's dead, and don't you say anything about her to me!" replied Oliver, a tear rolling down his cheek.

"She was a nice 'un, she was, your mother," continued Noah.

"But yer must know, Work'us, yer mother was a regular bad 'un."

"What did you say?"

"A regular bad 'un, your mother was. Lucky she died when she did, or else she'd be in prison or hung or something."

Crimson with fury, Oliver knocked over the chair and table, seized Noah by the throat, shook him until the teeth chattered in his head

and with one tremendous blow knocked him to the ground.

"Help! Help! Oliver's gone mad!" blubbered Noah. "He'll murder me! Help! Char-lotte!"

Noah's shouts were answered by a loud scream from Charlotte, who rushed into the kitchen, and seizing Oliver began beating him with her fists.

"You mur-de-rous, hor-rid little vil-lain!" she screamed and continued punching the poor child while Noah, who had at last risen from the ground, pommelled him from behind.

The noise and commotion at last roused Mrs Sowerberry who, on entering the kitchen and seeing the proceedings, joined in the fray. When at last they were all three wearied out they dragged Oliver back to the workhouse where Mr Bumble administered yet another thrashing on poor Oliver.

It was not until he was alone in the silence and stillness of his gloomy room, that Oliver gave way to his feelings. When there was no one to see him, he fell down on his knees and, hiding his face in his hands, wept bitterly.

For a long time after his tears had ceased, he remained motionless in this position. Then, looking cautiously round, he quietly crept down the stairs, gently unfastened the front door and peered outside.

The night was cold and dark. Softly, he closed the door and was in the open street. Looking right and left, he followed the road out of town until he came to a footpath leading across some fields. Then, creeping under a hay-rick he lay down and fell fast asleep.

3 Fagin's Gang

The next morning Oliver awoke cold and stiff and so hungry that he was forced to exchange his only penny for a small loaf of bread in the very first village he came to. He had walked no more than twelve miles, when night closed in again. Another night spent in the bleak damp air, made him feel so cold and ill that when he started his journey next morning, he could hardly crawl along.

At last, at the bottom of a steep hill, a stage-coach came along. Desperately, Oliver implored the driver and the outside passengers to stop. But no one took any notice of him. Exhausted as he was, poor Oliver ran alongside the coach a little way before falling, with bleeding feet, on to the rough, wet road. And there he would have remained for ever but for a kindly road-worker who gave him some bread and cheese.

Refreshed, Oliver continued his journey to London. In some villages, large painted signs were fixed up warning all persons who begged that they would be sent to jail. This made Oliver very frightened and glad to be out of them. If he begged at a farmer's house, the dog was set on him, and if he dared show his nose in a shop or at an inn he was threatened with the beadle.

In fact, had it not been for a benevolent old lady who gave him what little she could afford — and more — Oliver's troubles would have most assuredly have ended by his falling dead upon the road.

Early in the seventh morning after he had left Mr Sowerberry's, Oliver limped slowly into the

little town of Barnet on the edge of London. The window-shutters were closed; the street was empty. With bleeding feet and covered in dust, Oliver sat down on a doorstep. After a while the shutters were opened and people began passing to and fro. A few stopped to gaze at Oliver for a moment or two, or turned round to stare at him as they hurried on. But none troubled themselves to ask how he came to be there or to offer him any help. And he had no heart to beg. So he just sat there.

He had been crouching on the step for some time when he noticed the queerest-looking boy he had ever seen staring at him from the opposite side of the street. Though he was a boy of about Oliver's age, he had about him all the airs and manners of a man. Crossing the road, the boy walked up to Oliver and said, " 'Allo, my covey, what's up?"

"I'm very hungry and tired," returned Oliver, tears standing in his eyes as he spoke. "I've walked a very long way. I've been walking for seven days."

"Walkin' fer sivin days! Goin' to London, I 'sp'ose."

"Yes."

"Got any lodgings?"

"No."

"Money?"

"No."

The strange boy whistled. "Well don't fret yer eyelids on that score, young 'un. I know an old gentlemen in London wot'll give you lodgings for nothink."

The offer of shelter was too tempting to resist, especially as it was followed by the suggestion that they eat first. So, with his new friend, who introduced himself as Jack Dawkins, otherwise known as the Artful Dodger, Oliver was taken to a nearby shop and was bought bread and ham and then, at the direction of the Artful Dodger, they proceeded to an inn where a pot of beer was consumed by each.

It was nightfall when they eventually reached the street where the old gentleman lived. And a dirtier or more wretched place Oliver had never

seen. In fact, he was just wondering whether he had not better run away when his companion suddenly said, " 'ere we are, Oliver!" He gave a shrill whistle and thumped on the door three times. "Come on, Fagin, let us in!"

A pair of bespectacled eyes appeared through a grate at the top of the door.

"There's two of you," stated a cold, thin voice. "Who's the other one?"

"A new pal, Oliver Twist."

The heavy old door creaked slowly open. "Fagin, this is 'im. Oliver Twist."

Fagin was an old man with a thick, flowing beard, long grey hair, and a pair of spectacles perched on the end of his nose. Taking Oliver by his cold, limp hand, he said, "Pleased to meet you, Oliver, I'm sure. Very pleased indeed."

Oliver was led up a dark and broken staircase to a small back room. The walls and ceiling were black with age and dirt. The room was hot and

stuffy. A bare table stood in front of a bright fire. Several rough beds were huddled side by side on the floor. Seated round the table were four or five boys, none older than the Dodger.

"Dodger, our friend is hungry. Get him something to eat. Sit down, Oliver. You can watch us play a little game while you eat."

"Thank you, sir."

At this the other boys burst into boisterous laughter, but Oliver sat down as he had been told and ate his supper.

Fagin's little game began at once. First he placed a snuff-box in one pocket of his trousers, then a notebook in the other, and finally a gold watch inside his waistcoat. Then, buttoning up his jacket very tightly round him, he trotted up and down the room waving a stick — like an old gentleman walking about the streets in broad daylight.

Sometimes he stopped at the fireplace and sometimes at the door, pretending to be looking attentively into shop windows. At such times he would suddenly swing round, looking for thieves. Then he would tap all his pockets in turn, to make sure he had not lost anything. And he did it in such a funny and natural way that Oliver laughed until the tears ran down his face.

All this time two boys followed him closely, the Dodger and Charley Bates, getting out of his sight, so nimbly, every time he turned round, that it was impossible to follow their motions. At last the Dodger trod on Fagin's toes, while Charley stumbled up against him from behind; and in that one moment they took from him, with the most extraordinary speed, snuff-box, notebook, pocket-handkerchief, even his old

spectacle-case. If the old gentleman felt a hand in any of his pockets, he cried out where it was and then the game began all over again.

When this game had been played a great many times, Fagin said, "Well done, boys, well done. Enough for one day. I think it's time young Oliver got some sleep!"

It was late the next morning when he woke. There was no one in the room but Fagin. Half asleep, Oliver watched as Fagin took a small box from under the floorboards and placed it carefully on the table. Then, looking anxiously all around, Fagin took out rings, brooches, bracelets and other precious jewels.

Staring round, his eye fell on Oliver's face. The boy's eyes were fixed on him in terror. With a crash, Fagin closed the lid of the box and, laying his hand on a bread knife from the table, he shouted furiously,

"What's this? What do you watch me for? Why are you awake? What have you seen? Speak out, boy! Quick — quick! For your life!"

"I wasn't able to sleep any longer, sir. I'm very sorry if I disturbed you."

"Hmm, did you see any of the pretty things?" asked Fagin, laying his hand on the box.

"Yes, sir."

"Well, now! They — they're mine, Oliver. All mine. Something to live on in my old age. Folks call me a miser. And that's what I am. Only a miser. Now, get up, Oliver, I've a little job for you to do when the Dodger and Charley return."

Later that morning the three boys set out.

They had been walking a long time, when, just as they were emerging from a narrow court not far from Clerkenwell Green, the Dodger suddenly stopped.

"See that old cove at the bookstall?" he asked, pointing to an old gentleman across the road. "He'll do!"

Before Oliver had time to say anything, the Dodger and Charley were across the road and close behind the old gentleman. And to Oliver's utter horror, he saw the Dodger plunge his hand into the old gentleman's pocket, draw out a handkerchief and hand it to Charley.

In an instant the whole business of the handkerchiefs and the watches and the jewels and Fagin's little game became clear. Confused and frightened, Oliver took to his heels. But at that very moment the old gentleman, putting his hand in his pocket and missing his handkerchief, turned round. Seeing Oliver start to run away at such speed, he began shouting, "Stop, thief!" with all his might.

Immediately, a crowd joined in the chase, crying, "Stop, thief! Stop that boy!" Soon their cry was taken up by a hundred voices. After poor Oliver they ran, splashing through the mud and

rattling along the pavements; up went the windows; out ran the people, until, panting with exhaustion, a look of terror in his eyes and perspiration streaming down his face, Oliver was finally felled by a mighty blow.

Jostling and pushing, the crowd gathered round. "Stand aside there! Make way for the gentleman, do!" said the man who knocked Oliver down.

At that moment a police officer made his way through the crowd, and seized Oliver by the collar.

"Is this the boy what robbed you, sir?" asked the police officer.

"I'm afraid it is," replied the old gentleman.

"Afraid! Afraid!" murmured the policeman. "That's a good 'un. Come on, get up!" he said roughly.

"Please, sir, it wasn't me, it was two other boys. They're here somewhere," said Oliver, looking round wildly.

"Come on, you young devil, I've heard that one before. Come on, get up!"

And Oliver, who could hardly stand, was dragged along by his collar at a rapid pace with the gentleman by the officer's side.

"It's Mr Fang the magistrate for you, my lad," said the policeman. "And don't expect any sympathy from him! 'Cos you won't get any."

Indeed he was right. When Mr Fang looked at Oliver when he appeared in court, he gave him an angry scowl. The gentleman bowed respectfully.

"Who are you?" asked Mr Fang, angrily.

"My name, sir," said the man, "is Brownlow."

"Officer! What's this man charged with?"

"He's not charged with anything at all, your worship," replied the officer. "He appears against the boy."

"Appears against the boy, does he?" said Mr Fang, surveying Mr Brownlow contemptuously from head to foot. "Swear him in!"

"Before I am sworn, I must beg . . ."

"Hold your tongue, you insolent, impertinent fellow. How dare you bully a magistrate! I'll have you turned out! Swear this person!" he said turning to the clerk, "I'll not hear another word!"

Reluctantly Mr Brownlow was sworn in.

"Now," said Fang, "what's the charge against the boy? What have you got to say, sir?"

"I was standing at a bookstall . . ." began Mr Brownlow.

"Hold your tongue, sir!" said Mr Fang. "Policeman! Where's that policeman. Now, policeman, what is all this?"

The policeman related how he had taken the charge; how he had searched Oliver and found nothing and that was all he knew.

"Any other witnesses?"

"None, your worship."

"Now, state your complaint against this boy," he said, turning to Mr Brownlow, "or I'll punish you for disrespect to the bench!"

With many interruptions and repeated insults, Mr Brownlow described what he had seen and concluded by saying that he hoped the boy would be dealt with leniently. "He has been hurt already and I really fear that he is very ill."

"Oh, I dare say he is!" replied Mr Fang with a

sneer. "Come now, none of your tricks, you young vagabond. What's your name?"

Oliver tried to reply, but his tongue failed him. He was deadly pale and the whole place seemed to be turning round and round.

"What's your name, you little scoundrel?"

Oliver raised his hand and, looking round, fell heavily to the floor in a faint.

"I knew he was pretending," said Mr Fang. "Let him lie there, he'll soon tire of that."

"How do you propose to deal with the case, sir?" inquired the clerk in a low voice.

"Severely," replied Mr Fang. "He stands committed for three months — hard labour, of course, Clear the court!"

"Stop! Stop! Don't take him away!" cried a man who burst into the courtroom at that very moment, breathless with haste.

"What's this? Who is this person? Clear the court!"

"I saw it all. I keep the bookstall. You must hear me, Mr Fang. I demand to be sworn in!"

"Swear the fellow," growled Fang, reluctantly. "Now, man, what have you to say?"

"I saw three boys: two others and the prisoner, loitering on the opposite side of the street, while this gentleman was reading. But the robbery was committed by another boy. I saw it done."

"You're absolutely certain this is not the culprit?" demanded Mr Fang.

"The boy is innocent!"

"Huh! Pity! Looks like a criminal to me. Case dismissed. Clear the court!"

The court was cleared as directed. Little Oliver Twist was thrown onto the pavement outside. His face was deadly white and a cold trembling convulsed his whole frame.

"Poor boy, poor boy!" said Mr Brownlow, bending over him. "Call a coach, somebody, directly!"

"May I accompany you?" asked the bookstall-keeper.

"Bless me, yes, of course, my dear friend," replied Mr Brownlow. "Jump in. There's no time to lose, poor fellow!"

The bookstall-keeper got into the coach and away they drove.

4 Kidnapped

"Why, how's this?" muttered Fagin, as the Dodger and Charley Bates returned to his house. "Where's Oliver? Where's the boy?"

The two young thieves eyed Fagin sheepishly, but said nothing.

"What's become of the boy?" asked Fagin again, grabbing the Dodger tightly by the collar. "Speak or I'll throttle you!"

"The police got 'im, and that's all about it!" replied the Dodger. "Let me go, will yer?"

And swinging himself free, he picked up a toasting-fork and lunged at Fagin. But with greater agility than one would expect from such a decrepi old man, Fagin skipped back and, seizing up a pot, hurled it at the Dodger.

"Oi, who pitched that 'ere at me?" demanded a deep voice. "Wot's this all about?" The man who growled out these words was stoutly-built with a broad, heavy face and two scowling eyes. Behind him skulked his bull terrier, Bullseye.

"What you up to, Fagin? Ill-treating the boys again, heh? I wonder they don't murder you: I would if I was them!"

"Well, well, Bill Sikes," said Fagin. "You seem out of humour, Bill."

"Perhaps I am," replied Sikes. "I should think *you* was rather out of sorts yourself, throwing pewter pots about the place."

After a while, when all was calm, the Dodger related to Sikes and Fagin the circumstances of Oliver's capture.

"I'm afraid," said Fagin, "that he may say something which will get us into trouble."

"Very likely," returned Sikes with a malicious grin. "You're done for, Fagin!"

"And I'm afraid," added Fagin, looking at Sikes closely, "that if the game was up with me, it might be up with a good many more, and that it would be rather worse for you than it would for me, my dear."

Sikes turned with a fierce look on his face. There was a long pause. "Somebody must find out wot's been done to Oliver," he said finally.

Fagin nodded assent.

"If he hasn't already squealed against us, that is. You must get hold of him, Fagin."

Again Fagin nodded. It was obvious that none of them could go to the police station to find out what had happened to Oliver. But their dilemma was answered by the arrival of Sikes' friend, Nancy.

"Nancy, my dear," said Fagin in a soothing manner, after explaining what he wanted her to do, "What do you say?"

"That it won't do, so it's no use a-trying it on, Fagin."

"She'll go, Fagin, don't you worry," said Sikes. And he was right. After threatening her

with a beating if she refused, Nancy agreed to do as Fagin asked.

So, with a clean apron tied over her dress and her hair tucked up under a straw bonnet, Nancy made her way to the police station.

"Is there a little boy here?" she asked the police officer behind the desk, with a sob. "My poor, dear, sweet little brother! What ever has become of him? Have pity, sir, please. Tell me what's been done to my poor little brother."

"No need to carry on, miss," replied the policeman, kindly. "We haven't got him."

"Haven't got him?" screamed Nancy. "Wherever is he? Oh my poor, dear brother!"

"Why, the gentleman's got him," replied the policeman; and he proceeded to tell Nancy that Oliver had been taken to a house somewhere in Pentonville.

"We must know where he is, my dears," said Fagin when Nancy returned. "He *must* be found. Charley, do nothing till you bring news of him! Nancy, my dear, I must have him found.

I trust to you and the Artful for everything! But wait a moment," he added, unlocking a drawer with shaking hand, "there's money. Don't stop here a minute. Not an instant, my dears! Find him out, that's all! I shall know what to do next, never fear."

And with these words he pushed them from the room and carefully double-locked and barred the door. "He hasn't squealed so far," said Fagin. "If he means to blab among his new friends, we may stop his mouth yet."

Meanwhile, Oliver was recovering in Mr Brownlow's neat house in a shady street near Pentonville. For many days after his arrival, Oliver remained insensible to all the goodness of his new friends. Weak and thin and pallid, he awoke at last from what seemed to have been a long and troubled dream.

"What room is this?" he asked. "Where am I."

"Hush, my dear," replied Mrs Bedwin, Mr Brownlow's housekeeper. "You must be very

quiet, or you will be ill again. Lie down, there's a dear!" With these words the old lady gently placed Oliver's head upon the pillow and smoothed back his hair.

So Oliver kept very still, and soon fell into a gentle doze. He was awakened by the light of a candle. A gentleman with a very large and loud-ticking gold watch in his hand was feeling his pulse and said that Oliver was a great deal better.

Within three days he was able to sit in a chair, well propped up with pillows. Too weak to walk, Mrs Bedwin had him carried downstairs into her own little room, where he was brought some tea by the fireside.

"You're very, very, kind to me, ma'am," said Oliver.

"Well, never you mind that, my dear. Just drink your tea," replied the old lady, sitting down.

Oliver had scarcely finished when there was a soft tap on the door.

"Come in," said Mrs Bedwin, and in walked Mr Brownlow.

"How do you feel, Oliver?"

"Very happy, sir. And very grateful indeed, for your goodness to me."

"Good boy," said Mr Brownlow, stoutly.

"Why! Good heavens! What's this? Bedwin, look there!"

As he spoke, Mr Brownlow pointed to a picture above Oliver's head and then to the boy's face. There was its living copy. The eyes, the head, the mouth; every feature was the same!

Nothing, however, was said to Oliver about the picture. Indeed, on Mr Brownlow's instructions it was removed from the room and stored away.

One evening, about a week after the incident of the picture, as he was sitting talking to Mrs Bedwin, there came a message from Mr Brownlow that if Oliver felt well he should like to see him in his study.

Oliver tapped at the study door. As he entered the room, he saw Mr Brownlow sitting at a table by a window, reading.

"Now," he said in a kind but serious manner. "I want you to pay great attention, my boy, to what I am going to say."

"Oh, don't tell me you are going to send me away, sir! Don't turn me out of doors to wander in the streets. Don't send me back to that wretched place I came from. Have mercy upon a poor boy, sir!"

"My dear child you need not be afraid of my deserting you, unless you give me cause."

"I never will, sir. Never!"

"I hope not. Now, Oliver . . ."

Just then an impatient double-knock was heard at the street door and the servant, running up the stairs, announced Mr Grimwig.

"Hallo! Who's that!" said Mr Grimwig as he entered the study and saw Oliver.

"This is young Oliver Twist, whom we were speaking about," replied Mr Brownlow.

As fate would have it, Mrs Bedwin happened to come it at that moment with a small parcel of books, which a messenger from the bookstall had just delivered.

"Stop the boy, Mrs Bedwin!" said Mr Brownlow. "There's something I want him to take back."

"He's gone, sir."

"Send Oliver with them," suggested Mr Grimwig with a malicious grin, "he'll be sure to deliver them safely, you know."

"What an excellent idea! Oliver, fetch the books for me, would you please?"

Delighted to be of some use, Oliver did as he was asked, and waited cap in hand to hear the message he was to take.

"You are to say," said Mr Brownlow, glancing steadily at Mr Grimwig, "that you have brought the books back and that you have come to pay the five pounds I owe. Is that clear?"

"Yes sir, I won't be ten minutes," replied Oliver eagerly.

"Bless his sweet face." said Mrs Bedwin as soon as Oliver had gone. "I can't bear to let him out of my sight."

"He'll be back in twenty minutes at the latest," said Mr Brownlow.

"You really expect him back, do you?" inquired Mr Grimwig.

"Don't you?" asked Mr Brownlow, smiling.

"No. I do not. The boy has a new suit of clothes on his back, a set of valuable books under his arm and a five-pound note in his pocket. He'll join his old friends the thieves and laugh at you. If ever that boy returns to this house, sir, I'll eat my hat!"

cried Oliver struggling in Sikes' powerful grasp. "Help! Help!"

"I'll soon stop your nonsense, my lad!" exclaimed Bill Sikes. And with these words he tore the books from Oliver's hands and struck him on the head. Then, seizing Oliver by the scruff of his neck, he gave him another blow for good measure. "Come on, you young villain!" he said and dragged the boy into a maze of dark narrow streets and alleys.

"Delighted to see you looking so well, my dear," said Fagin when they arrived. "Why didn't you write and say you were coming? We'd have got something warm for supper."

At this everyone roared with laughter.

"Look at 'is togs, Fagin," shouted Charley Bates, "and 'is books! Wot a gentleman! Oh my eye, what a game!"

"We're delighted to see you looking so well, me dear," said Fagin, bowing in mock humility. "But the Artful had better give you another suit of clothes, for fear you should spoil that nice one."

"They're very pretty," said Charley Bates, picking up the books and pretending to read one of them. "Beautiful writing, isn't it Oliver?" And at this he fell into another bout of boisterous laughter.

"But they belong to the gentleman," said Oliver, wringing his hands. "He'll think I stole them, and so will Mrs Bedwin. All of them who were so kind to me will think I stole them. Have mercy on me and send them back! Please!"

With these words Oliver fell on his knees at Fagin's feet and beat his hands together in

Earlier that same day, in an obscure back room of a public house in the filthiest part of London, Bill Sikes sat brooding over a tankard of ale muttering to Fagin, who sat very ill at ease.

As he spoke, Nancy dressed in bonnet and shawl, burst into the room and said, "The brat's been ill and confined to the house, and . . ."

"After him, Nancy," said Fagin. "He'll have to go out some time. And Bill, you go with Nancy — you may be needed."

Pulling her shawl over her shoulders, Nancy left with Bill Sikes who was followed, at a little distance, by Bullseye.

Meanwhile Oliver, little dreaming that he was within so very short a distance of Fagin, was on his way to the bookstall. He was walking along thinking how happy he was when he was startled by a young woman screaming out very loud, "Oh, me dear brother!" He had hardly looked up when he was stopped by a pair of arms grabbing him tight round the neck.

"I've found him! Oh! Oliver! You naughty boy, to make me suffer such distress . . ."

"Don't," cried Oliver, struggling and kicking. "Let go of me. What are you doing?"

Nancy had caused such a commotion that a small crowd had gathered.

"What's the matter," shouted a woman, "what's going on here?"

"It's me brother Oliver. He ran away from home and almost broke his mother's heart."

"Go home to yer poor mother, you little brute!" shouted Bill Sikes, bursting out of a beer-shop.

"I don't belong to them. I don't know them."

wild desperation.

"You're right, Oliver, you're right. They *will* think you have stolen 'em. Ha! Ha! Ha! it couldn't have happened better!" chuckled Fagin, rubbing his hands.

"Of course it couldn't," replied Sikes. "I know'd that directly I see him coming along with those books under his arm. And them wot kept 'im won't ask no questions arter him for fear they should be obliged to prosecute and so get him hanged. He's safe enough now."

At these words Oliver jumped suddenly to his feet and tore wildly round the room uttering shrieks for help which made the bare old house echo to the roof.

"Wanted to get assistance, call the police, did you?" sneered Fagin, catching Oliver by the arm. "We'll cure you of that, my young friend." And he inflicted a smart blow on Oliver's

shoulders with a club that knocked him to the floor. He was just raising it for a second blow when Nancy rushed forward, grabbed it from his hand and flung it into the fire.

"I won't stand by and see it done, Fagin," she cried. "You've got the boy, what more do you want? Let him be — or I'll do something to you that'll bring you to the gallows!"

"Why Nancy!" said Fagin after a pause, during which he and Sikes had stared hard at one another, "You wouldn't do a thing like that, would you? Not to Bill and me surely?"

"Wouldn't I! Take care I don't! You'll be the worse for it Fagin, if I do. So I'm telling you to keep clear of me."

All this time poor Oliver just lay on the floor. Too feeble to resist, he was picked up by Bill Sikes and thrown into another room, where feeling sick and weary, he sank into unconsciousness.

5 The Evidence Destroyed

In the very same town in which Oliver Twist was born, Mr Bumble emerged early one morning from the workhouse-gate and walked with portly carriage and commanding steps up the High Street. He was in the full bloom and pride of beadlehood; and with his head held even higher than usual, Mr Bumble boarded the London coach.

Again and again throughout the journey his eye rested on the following newspaper advertisement

> ### FIVE GUINEAS REWARD
> The above reward will be paid to any person who will give information as will lead to the discovery of a young boy named Oliver Twist or throw any light upon his previous history.

Then followed a full description of Oliver's dress, appearance and disappearance, with the name and address of Mr Brownlow.

Arriving in London, Mr Bumble, after consuming a modest dinner of steaks and oysters and ale, proceeded to Mr Brownlow's house in Pentonville.

"Come in, come in," said Mrs Bedwin when Mr Bumble had stated his errand. "I knew we should hear of him. Poor dear! I knew we should. Bless his heart! I said so all along."

Having said this the old lady showed Mr

Bumble into the little back study, where sat Mr Brownlow and his friend Mr Grimwig, who at once burst into the exclamation:

"A beadle! A parish beadle, or I'll eat my hat!"

"I *am* a parish beadle," replied Mr Bumble.

"You come in response to the advertisement?" asked Mr Brownlow, impatiently.

"Yes, sir."

"Do you know where this poor boy is now?"

"No more than nobody," replied Mr Bumble none too helpfully.

"Well, what *do* you know of him? Speak out my friend, if you have anything to say. What do you know of him?"

Mr Bumble put down his hat, unbuttoned his coat, folded his arms and after a few moments reflection, commenced his story.

". . . Therefore, sir, to sum up," said Mr Bumble after having spoken for some twenty minutes, "Oliver Twist is, in my long and bitter experience, treacherous, ungrateful and malicious. He ran away from his master's house after a cowardly and vicious attack on the innocent, helpless lad, Noah Claypole . . . and this after

causing a riot in the workhouse. In short, he's a hardened criminal."

Mr Brownlow paced the room for some minutes, much disturbed by the beadle's tale. At length he ran the bell violently. "I fear it is all too true," he said sorrowfully. "Here is your reward. I would gladly have given you treble if it had been favourable to the boy."

"Mrs Bedwin," he continued when the housekeeper answered his call, "Oliver is an imposter. Never let me hear the boy's name mentioned again. Never!

"He was a dear, grateful, gentle child," retorted Mrs Bedwin, bursting into tears. "I *know* what children are, sir, and have done these forty years."

"You may leave the room, Mrs Bedwin. And remember! I am in earnest."

There were sad hearts at Mr Brownlow's that night after the beadle had left.

On returning home, Mr Bumble walked back up the High Street until he came to a public house. It began to rain heavily at that moment. This determined him. Mr Bumble stepped in and ordering something to drink entered the parlour, which was deserted save for one solitary customer.

The man who was seated there was tall and dark and wore a large cloak. He had the air of a stranger and by the mud and dust on his coat seemed to have travelled some distance. After having encountered each other's glance several times, the stranger, in a harsh, deep voice, broke the silence.

"I have seen you before, I think," he said. "You are beadle here, are you not?"

"I am the parish beadle, yes," replied Mr Bumble.

The stranger smiled, and nodded his head, as much as to say, he had not mistaken his man.

"Now listen to me," he said, "I came down to this place today to find you out. I want some information from you. I don't ask you to give it for nothing, slight as it is." And as he spoke he pushed two sovereigns across the table.

"Carry your memory back — let me see — some twelve years."

"It's a long time," said Mr Bumble. "Very good. I've done it."

"The scene, the workhouse."

"Good!"

"And the time, night."

"Yes."

"And the place, the lying-in room where a boy was born."

"Many boys," observed Mr Bumble, shaking his head.

"I speak of one: a meek-looking, pale-faced devil who was apprenticed to a coffin-maker and who afterwards ran away to London."

"Why, you mean Oliver Twist!" said Mr Bumble. "I remember him of course. There wasn't a worse . . ."

"It's not of him I want to hear. It's of a woman: the hag that nursed his mother. Where is she?"

"She died last winter. My wife was with her when she died and she could, I believe, throw some light on the subject, should you be interested . . ."

"When?" asked the stranger, hastily.

"Tomorrow," rejoined Mr Bumble.

"At nine in the evening," said the stranger, producing a scrap of paper and writing on it an address. "At nine in the evening, bring her to me there. I needn't tell you to be secret. It's in your own interest."

With these words he led the way to the door, stopping only to pay for what they had drunk. Glancing at the address, Mr Bumble saw that it contained no name. The stranger had not gone far, so he made after him.

"What name am I to ask for?" he said, touching the man on the arm.

"Monks!" answered the man and strode quickly away.

It was a dull, close, overcast summer evening that threatened a violent thunder-storm, when Mr and Mrs Bumble directed their course towards the ruined house erected on a low unwholesome swamp, bordering on the river.

As they stood before this building, the first peal of distant thunder reverberated in the air and the rain poured violently down.

"Hallo there!" cried a voice from above.

Following the sound, Mr Bumble raised his head and saw a man looking out of a door on the second storey.

"Is that the man?" asked Mrs Bumble.

Mr Bumble nodded.

"Then, mind what I told you," she said, "and be careful you say as little as possible, or you'll betray us at once."

"Now," said Monks, when they had all three seated themselves, "the sooner we come to business the better. You were with the hag the night she died and she told you something?" he asked, turning to Mrs Bumble.

"About the mother of the boy you named, yes."

"The first question is, what did she say?"

"That's the second," observed the woman. "The first is, what's it worth?"

"It may be nothing, it may be twenty pounds. Who the devil can say without knowing what you've got to say?"

"Add five pounds to the sum you named. Give me five-and-twenty pounds and I'll tell you all I know."

"Five-and-twenty pounds!" exclaimed Monks.

Reluctantly, he thrust his hand into a side pocket and, producing a canvas bag, counted out twenty-five pounds on the table and pushed

33

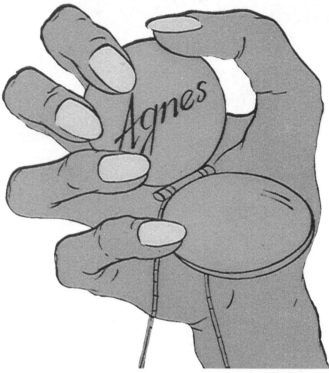

them over to Mrs Bumble. Just then a peal of thunder seemed to shake the whole house. Raising his head, Monks bent forward to listen to what she had to say.

"When this woman, that we called old Sally, died, she and I were alone. She spoke of a young woman who had brought a child into the world some years before. The child was the one you named last night to him," and she nodded towards Mr Bumble. "This young mother, old Sally robbed. She stole from the corpse something the young mother had asked her, with her last breath, to keep for her child."

"She sold it?" cried Monks. "Did she sell it? Where? When? To whom? How long ago?"

"As old Sally told me, with great difficulty, that she had done this, she fell back and died."

"It's a lie!" screamed Monks. "She said more. I'll tear the life out of you both, if you don't tell me!"

"She didn't utter another word," said Mrs Bumble quite unmoved, "but she clutched my gown, violently, with her hand, which was partly closed. And when I saw that she was dead, I removed the hand with force and found that it clasped a scrap of dirty paper."

"Which contained . . .?" asked Monks, stretching forward.

"Nothing. Just a pawnbroker's ticket."

"For what?" demanded Monks.

"There!" replied the woman. And, as if glad

to be relieved of it, she threw down a small leather purse, which Monks, pouncing upon, tore open with trembling hands. It contained a little gold locket in which the name 'Agnes' was engraved.

"And this is all?" asked Monks.

"All. Is it what you expected to get from me?"

"It is."

"What do you propose to do with it? Can it be used against me?" demanded Mrs Bumble.

"Never," answered Monks, "nor against me neither. See here! But don't move a step forward!"

With these words, he suddenly wheeled the table aside and, pulling an iron ring in the boarding, threw back a large trap-door, which opened close to Mr Bumble's feet and caused him to retire several paces backwards.

"Look down," said Monks, lowering the lantern. "Don't fear me. I could have let you down, quietly enough, when you were seated over it, if that had been my game."

The two looked down at the turbid water, swollen by the heavy rain, rushing rapidly below. Monks drew the gold locket from his pocket where he had hurriedly placed it, and dropped it into the stream. The three, looking into each other's faces, seemed to breathe more freely.

"Now light your lantern and get away from here, as fast as you can," said Monks. They left in silence. Monks brought up the rear, after pausing to satisfy himself that there were no other sounds to be heard, than the beating of the rain and the rushing of the water.

6 The Burglary

It was about noon the next day when Oliver awoke. The Dodger and Charley Bates had gone out. Oliver was alone in the house with Fagin, who took the opportunity of lecturing the boy on the sin of ingratitude. Smiling hideously, he patted Oliver on the head and said that if he kept himself quiet and applied himself to learning the "business" then he saw no reason why the two of them should not be friends. Then, taking up his hat, he departed, locking the door behind him.

And so Oliver remained all that day, and for the great part of many subsequent days; seeing nobody between early morning and midnight. After the lapse of a week or so, Fagin left the room-door unlocked. From that day Oliver was seldom left alone, but was placed in the constant company of the Dodger and Bates, who for Oliver's benefit, played the old handkerchief game with Fagin.

At other times Fagin would tell them stories of robberies he had committed in his younger days, mixed up with stories so droll and curious that Oliver could not help laughing heartily and showing that he was amused in spite of his better feelings. Thus Fagin prepared Oliver's mind, by solitude and gloom, to prefer any company to that of his own sad thoughts in such a dreary place.

Thus Oliver spent several weeks after his capture. Then, waking one morning, he was surprised to see a new pair of shoes, with strong, thick soles, placed beside his bed. At first he thought that it meant he might be released, a thought soon dispelled by Fagin telling him that he was to take up residence with Bill Sikes, that very evening.

"To . . . to . . . stop there, sir?" asked Oliver.

"No, no, my dear. Not to stop there. We shouldn't like to lose you. Don't be afraid, Oliver, you shall come back to us. Ha! ha! ha!"

Late that afternoon, alone in the house, Oliver heard a knock on the door.

"What's that! Who's there?"

"Me. Only me," replied a voice.

Oliver raised the candle above his head and looked towards the door. It was Nancy.

"Put down the light," said the girl. "It hurts my eyes. I've come from Bill. Come on, you're to go with me."

She took the hand which Oliver instinctively placed in hers, and, blowing out the light, quickly opened the door and passed into the street.

"This way," she said after they had been walking for some time, "in, 'ere." And she pushed Oliver into a dark passageway.

"So you've got the kid," said Sikes, appearing at the top of a steep flight of stairs.

"Yes, here he is," replied Nancy.

"Come here young 'un and let me tell you

something which is well got over at once."

Pulling Oliver into a gloomy room, he snatched his cap off his head and, taking up a pistol, said, "Know wot this is?"

"Yes, please, sir."

"Well then, look here. This is powder; that 'ere's a bullet and this is a little bit of old hat for waddin'."

Carefully, Sikes loaded the pistol. Then he grasped Oliver's wrist tightly and put the barrel so close to his temple that they touched. "If you speak a word when you're out o' doors with me, except when I speak to you, that loading will be in your head without notice. So if you *do* make up your mind to speak without leave, say your prayers first."

For a long time Oliver lay awake that night weary, wretched and afraid, while Nancy sat brooding over the fire and Sikes drank and cursed.

"Now then!" growled Sikes the next morning, "it's half-past five! Look sharp or you'll get no breakfast; its late as it is."

It was a cheerless morning when they got into the street, blowing and raining hard. There were few out of doors in that part of town, for the

"I'm your man as far as I go," he replied.

The night was very dark. A damp mist rose from the river. It was piercing cold too; all was black and gloomy. Oliver sat huddled in a corner of the cart, bewildered with alarm and apprehension. After what seemed to be many miles, the cart stopped. Sikes got out and, taking Oliver by the hand, began walking once again.

They hurried through the main street of a little town, then, quickening their pace, turned up a road and after walking abut a quarter of a mile, stopped before a large, detached house.

"Now," said Sikes, drawing the pistol from his pocket "if you don't do exactly what I say, I'll strew your brains on the grass! Now listen. I'm going to put you through there," and he pointed to a small lattice-window about five feet and a half above the ground. "When you're inside, go along the little hall to the street door, unbolt it and let me in. Right? And remember, no funny business. I'll have you covered."

This was no sooner said than Sikes forced open the window with his crowbar and pushed Oliver inside. In the short time he had had to collect his senses, Oliver decided that he would try to warn the people of the house, even if he were to die in the attempt. With this idea in mind he unbolted the front door, then made towards the stairs.

"Come back!" cried Sikes, "Back! back!"

Scared by the sudden breaking of the dead silence, Oliver tripped and fell. Suddenly, a light appeared and the vision of two terrified

windows were all closely shut and the streets through which they passed, were noiseless and empty.

As they approached the City of London the noise and traffic increased and as they headed south it swelled into a roar of sound and bustle. Sikes, dragging Oliver after him, elbowed his way through the thickest of the crowd.

"Come on, don't lag behind, already, lazy legs. There's miles to go yet."

And so they made their way through and across London with Oliver wondering more and more, as the day progressed, where Sikes was taking him. Kensington, Hammersmith, Chiswick, Kew Bridge, Brentford, were all passed and yet they went on as steadily as if their journey had just begun.

At length they turned into an old public house and ordered some dinner by the kitchen fire. They had some cold meat and, being tired with the walk and getting up so early, Oliver was soon dozing by the fire.

It was quite dark when he was awakened by a push from Sikes.

"Could you give my boy and me a lift?" he heard Sikes ask of a man sitting nearby.

half-dressed men at the top of the stairs swam before his eyes — a flash — a loud noise — smoke — a crash somewhere — and Oliver staggered back.

Sikes grabbed Oliver before the smoke had cleared away. He fired his own pistol after the men, who were already retreating, and dragged the boy out of the house.

"Clasp your arm tighter," said Sikes, then almost immediately, "My God, they've hit him. How the boy bleeds!"

Then came the loud ringing of a bell, mingled with the sound of pistol shots and the shouts of men. Oliver was lifted up and carried out of the house and over the ground at a rapid pace. And then the noises grew confused in the distance and a deadly cold crept over the boy, and he saw or heard no more.

There was little Sikes could see in the mist and darkness, but the loud shouting of men vibrated through the air and the barking of the neighbouring dogs, roused by the alarm bells, resounded in every direction. Sikes again looked round and could now see that the men giving chase were already climbing the gate of the field in which he stood; and that a couple of dogs were some paces in front of them.

Clenching his teeth he threw his cape over the body of Oliver; then, running along a hedge, he dived into the undergrowth and was gone.

The air grew colder as day came slowly on, and the mist rolled along the ground like a dense cloud of smoke. Still Oliver lay motionless and insensible on the spot where Sikes had left him. Morning drew on a pace. The air became sharp and piercing. Rain came down thick and fast, pattering noisily among the leafless bushes. But Oliver felt nothing as it beat against him; for he still lay outstretched, helpless and unconscious on his bed of clay.

At length, he awoke. His left arm hung heavy and useless at his side, his shirt saturated with blood. He was so weak he could scarcely raise himself. He groaned with pain. Every joint in his body trembled from cold and exhaustion. He made an effort to stand up, but shuddering from head to foot, he fell prostrate on the ground.

After a short time he got to his feet again. Staggering like a drunken man, he stumbled on, he knew not where. He looked about and saw at no great distance a house. As he drew nearer, a feeling came over him that he had seen it before. Then, suddenly, he remembered. It was the very same house he and Sikes had attempted to burgle. He pushed against the garden gate, tottered across the lawn, climbed the steps to the front door, then fainted.

Inside the kitchen, the servants heard a noise.

"Open the door," said Mr Giles.

"I will if you come with me," replied Brittles, who after his experience the previous night was still in a nervous state.

No sooner had Brittles opened the door and seen Oliver than he uttered a loud cry.

"A boy!" exclaimed Mr Giles, pushing Brittles into the background. "Why Brittles, look" and with this he seized Oliver by one leg and one arm and lugged him into the hall.

"What is it, Giles?" whispered a soft voice from the top of the stairs. "Hush, or you'll frighten my aunt!"

"It's one of the thieves, Miss Rose, wounded! I shot him, and Brittles held the light."

"Is the poor creature much hurt?" asked Rose as she came quietly down the stairs.

"Wounded desperate, miss. He looks as if he's a-going," replied Giles.

"Poor fellow! He's only a boy. Carry him upstairs, and Giles, treat him kindly, for my sake. Brittles — saddle the pony and go and get Dr Losberne, quick!"

7 A Strange Meeting

At length, and by slow degrees, under the united care of Rose, her aunt, Mrs Maylie, and the kind-hearted Dr Losberne, Oliver recovered from his wound and the fever that had hung about him for many weeks.

As he recovered, Oliver had told them about his life in the workhouse and about Fagin and Bill Sikes and the short period of happiness he had enjoyed at Mr Brownlow's. But it still troubled Oliver that Mr Brownlow and Mrs Bedwin did not know how grateful he had been to them for all their kindness. That they did not know what had happened to him on that fateful day when he had been kidnapped by Nancy and Sikes.

"If they knew how happy I am now, Mrs Maylie, they would be pleased I'm sure," said Oliver one day.

"I'm sure they would," Mrs Maylie replied, "and Dr Losberne has kindly promised that when you are well enough, he will take you to London to see them."

It was not long before Oliver was sufficiently recovered to undergo the journey, and one morning he and Dr Losberne set out in a little carriage belonging to Mrs Maylie. As Oliver knew the name of the street in which Mr Brownlow lived they drove straight there. When the coach finally turned into it, his heart beat so violently that he could scarcely draw his breath.

"Which house is it?" asked Dr Losberne.

"That one — there!" shouted Oliver, pointing to a neat, white house.

The coach rolled on. It stopped. No — that was the wrong house; the next door. It went on a few paces, and stopped again. But alas the house was empty; and there was a notice outside, which read 'To Let'.

Dr Losberne asked the neighbours what had become of Mr Brownlow. He was told that Mr Brownlow had sold off his possessions and left for the West Indies six weeks before with Mrs Bedwin and his friend Mr Grimwig.

The bitter disappointment caused Oliver much sorrow and grief. The idea that they should have gone so far, and carried with them

the belief that he was an imposter and a cheat and that they might think this until their dying day was almost more than he could bear.

Two weeks passed and with it the arrival of warm weather. The Maylie's began preparations for a visit to their country cottage. It was a lovely spot they went to with Oliver, and it was a happy time for the boy who had spent so much of his life in poverty and squalor. The days were peaceful and serene, the nights brought with them neither fear nor care. Every morning Oliver went to a white-headed old gentleman who lived near the little church and who taught him to read better and to write. So three months passed. Spring flew by, and summer came.

Throughout his stay Oliver occupied a little room on the ground floor, at the back of the house. It looked into a garden, beyond which were fine meadows and woods. One beautiful evening, when the first shades of twilight were beginning to settle upon the earth, Oliver sat at his window, reading a book. It had been a sultry day and Oliver, having been very active, sat there in the cool air gradually falling asleep.

He knew perfectly well that he was in his own little room; that his books were lying on the table before him. And yet he was asleep. Suddenly, the scene changed: the air became close and confined, and he thought with a glow of terror that he was in Fagin's house again. Fagin sat in his corner, pointing at him, and whispering to another man who sat beside him.

"Hush, my dear!" he thought he heard Fagin say, "It is he, sure enough. Come away."

"Do you think I wouldn't recognize him?" the

other man seemed to be saying. "If you buried him fifty feet deep and took me across his grave, I should know, if there wasn't a mark above it, that he lay buried there. I should!"

The man seemed to say this with such dreadful hatred that Oliver awoke terrified. But there, there at the window, close in front of him, so close that he could have touched him, with his eyes peering into the room and meeting his: there stood Fagin! And beside him, white with rage or fear or both, were the features of the man he had seen in his "dream".

It was but an instant, a flash before his eyes; then they were gone. But they had recognized him, and he them. He stood transfixed for a moment, and then, leaping from the window into the garden, called loudly for help.

"What direction did they take?" asked Giles.

"Over there," said Oliver, pointing in the direction of the meadows behind the house.

"Come on, Brittles, follow me and keep as close as you can. These men are dangerous."

Oliver followed and in the course of a minute or two Dr Losberne, who had been out walking,

joined them. But their search was in vain. There was not even the traces of recent footsteps to be seen. The four of them stood on the summit of a little hill, commanding a view of the open fields for three or four miles. There was no one.

"It *must* have been a dream, Oliver," said Dr Losberne.

"Oh no, indeed, sir," replied Oliver, "I saw them too plainly for that. I saw them both as plainly as I see you now."

And the earnest look on Oliver's face as he spoke convinced them all of the accuracy of what he said. Still, in no direction was there any sign of the trampling of men in hurried flight.

A further search was made the next day, but with no success. Enquiries were made in the local market town in the hope that someone had seen or heard something of the men, but this effort was equally fruitless, and after a few days the incident was almost forgotten.

Shortly after this the Maylie's went to London to stay for a few days in a quiet but handsome street near Hyde Park, accompanied, as usual, by Dr Losberne and Oliver.

On the second night after their arrival, in another, poorer part of town, Nancy hastily put on her bonnet and shawl, and looking fearfully round, crept quietly out of Bill Sikes' house and made her way to the West End of London.

The clock struck ten. She rushed along the narrow pavement until she reached the hotel where Miss Rose Maylie was staying.

"Now then, young woman," said the man at the door, "and what do you want here?"

"Miss Maylie, please, sir," answered Nancy, desperately. "You must let me speak with her. It's a matter of life or death!" The man, alarmed at the girl's appearance, ran up stairs. Pale and almost breathless, Nancy followed and entered the room. Seeing a slim and beautiful girl, she said, "I'm about to put my life and the lives of others in your hands. I am the girl that dragged little Oliver back to old Fagin's on the night he went out from the house in Pentonville."

"You!" said Rose Maylie.

"I, lady! But I have stolen away from those who would surely murder me if they knew I had been here, to tell you what I have overheard. Do you know of a man called Monks?"

"No," replied Rose.

"He knows you and knows you are here, for it was by hearing him tell the name of the place that I found you out."

"I never heard the name," said Rose, "who is he?"

"Well, some time ago and soon after Oliver was put into your house on the night of the robbery, I — suspecting this man Monks — listened to a conversation held between him and Fagin in the dark. I found out from what I heard that Monks had seen Oliver with two of our boys on the day we first lost him and recognized him as the same child that he was watching for, though I couldn't make out why. A bargain was struck with Fagin, that if he got Oliver back he should give him a certain sum of money, and he was to have more money for making him a thief which this Monks wanted for some purposes of his own."

"But for what purpose?" asked Rose.

"I don't know. I was afraid they might see me, so I left and didn't hear any more. And I saw him no more until tonight."

"And what happened then?"

"The first words I heard Monks say were these: 'So the only proof of the boy's identity lies at the bottom of the river and the old hag that got them from the boy's mother is rotting in her coffin.' They laughed and then Monks says that though he had got the young devil's money now, he'd rather see Oliver hauled before some court and imprisoned for some capital crime!"

"What is all this?" asked Rose.

"The truth, lady. 'In short, Fagin,' says he, 'you never laid such snares as I'll do for my young brother, Oliver'."

"His brother?" exclaimed Rose.

"Those were his very words," said Nancy. "Now it's growing late and I have to reach home without suspicion of having been here. I must get back quickly."

"This man Monks must be investigated," said Rose. "Where can I find you again when necessary?"

"Every Sunday night from eleven until the clock strikes twelve, I will walk on London Bridge — if I am alive."

Sobbing loudly, the unhappy Nancy turned away; while Rose, overpowered by the extraordinary interview, sank into a chair and tried to make some sense of what Nancy had said. Disturbed by these revelations, Rose passed a sleepless night. And with the new day, she was still in a quandary about what to do when Oliver came bursting into the room: "I have seen the gentleman, Mr Brownlow, who was so good to me!"

"Where?" asked Rose.

"Getting out of a coach and going into a house," replied Oliver. "I didn't speak to him — I couldn't speak to him, for he didn't see me. But Giles asked for me whether he lived there, and the servant said he did. Look here, here's the address," and he opened a scrap of paper.

"Quick," said Rose, "tell them to fetch a coach immediately and Oliver, be ready to go with me. I'll take you there directly."

In little more than five minutes they were on their way. And when they arrived, Rose left Oliver in the coach and saw Mr Brownlow privately.

"I shall surprise you very much, I have no doubt," she said to Mr Brownlow and another gentleman who was introduced to her as Mr Grimwig. "But you once showed great goodness to a very dear young friend, Oliver Twist, and I am sure you will take an interest in hearing of him again."

No sooner had the words escaped her lips than Mr Grimwig banged his fist on the table and growled, "A bad one! I knew that boy would come to no good. I'll eat my hat if he's not a bad one!"

"Do not heed my friend, Miss Maylie, he does not mean what he says. Now, tell me what you know of this poor child."

Rose at once, in a few simple words, told all that had befallen Oliver since he left Mr Brownlow's house, reserving only Nancy's information for Mr Brownlow's ear alone.

"Thank God the boy's safe and well!" said Mr Brownlow. "This is great happiness to me, great happiness. But where is he? Where is Oliver?"

"He's waiting in the coach outside."

"At this door?" Without another word, he hurried out of the room, down the stairs and into the coach.

"Send Mrs Bedwin here!" said Mr Brownlow, ringing his own front door bell.

"My dear old nurse!" cried Oliver.

"God be good to me!" cried the old lady. "It's my innocent boy! I knew he'd come back. How well he looks, how like a gentleman's son . . ."

Leaving Oliver and Mrs Bedwin to compare notes, Mr Brownlow led Rose into another room and there heard a full account of her interview with Nancy. Rose then explained that she had told no one else of what Nancy had said, not even Dr Losberne, for fear that he would not keep it a secret.

"We must meet Nancy on London Bridge as arranged," said Mr Brownlow, "and find out more about this Monks. Monks is the key to this mystery. Monks is behind everything!"

8 Fatal Consequences

On the very same night that Nancy, having lulled Bill Sikes to sleep, hurried to see Rose Maylie, there advanced towards London, by the Great North Road, two persons well acquainted with Oliver's history.

They toiled along the dusty road until they passed through Highgate, when the man stopped and called impatiently to his female companion,

"Come on, can't yer? What a lazy bones yer are, Charlotte."

"Is it much farther?" asked the girl, almost breathless with fatigue.

"Much farther! Yer as good as there," said Noah Claypole. "Look there! Those are the lights of London."

Through these streets Noah Claypole walked, dragging Charlotte after him. At length he stopped in front of a public house, dirtier and shabbier than any he had yet seen.

"The Three Cripples," he said, looking up at the sign. "Now then, keep close at my heels and come along!"

Charlotte obediently followed and together they entered the dingy house.

"We want to sleep here, tonight," said Noah, "and while you're at it give us some cold meat and a drop of beer, will yer?"

The two were ushered into a small back bar and refreshment brought to them. The landlord then went off to prepare their room and was just returning when Fagin, in the course of his evening's business, entered.

"Hush!" said the landlord, "there's strangers in the other room. They're robbers from the country."

Fagin heard this with great interest. Mounting a stool he looked through a small pane of glass into the bar where the two sat eating. "Yes," he whispered, "I like that fellow's looks.

He'll be one of us; he knows how to train the girl already. Don't make as much noise as a mouse, my dear, and let me hear 'em talk."

Fagin again applied his eye to the glass, and turning his ear to the partition, listened attentively.

"No more jolly old coffins, Charlotte," he heard Noah say, "but a gentleman's life for me my girl. And if yer like yer shall be a lady."

"I should like that well enough, dear," replied Charlotte, "but it won't always be as easy as it was robbing old Sowerberry's till."

"Tills be blowed! There's more things besides tills to be emptied. There's pockets, houses, mail-coaches, banks . . ."

He stopped suddenly as the door into the small bar opened and in walked Fagin.

"A pleasant night, sir, but cool for the time of year," he said, rubbing his hands. "From the country, I see, sir?"

" 'Ow d'you know that?" replied Noah.

"We have not so much dust as that in London," replied Fagin, pointing from Noah's shoes to those of his companion, and from them to two bundles.

"Yer a sharp feller," said Noah.

"Why, one needs to be sharp in this town, and that's the truth." And he beckoned the landlord to bring more drinks.

"Good stuff that," observed Mr Claypole, smacking his lips.

"My dear!" said Fagin, " 'A man needs to be always emptying a till, or a pocket, or a house, or a mail-coach, or a bank, if he drinks it regularly'."

No sooner had Noah heard his own words than he fell back in his chair, pale and terrified. "Don't mind me," said Fagin. "It was lucky it was only me that heard you. It was very lucky it was only me."

"I didn't take it," stammered Noah, "it was all her doing! It was Charlotte what done it."

"No matter who did it, my dear!" replied Fagin, "I'm in that way myself, and I like you for it."

"In what way?" asked Noah, innocently.

"In that way of business," rejoined Fagin, "and so are the people of the house. There's not a safer place in all this town for people like us, than The Three Cripples. And I'll tell you more. I have a friend who can gratify your wish and put you in the right way of business."

"I wouldn't mind something very light,"

admitted Noah. "Just to tide me over."

"A little fancy work, perhaps? Something in the spying line? My friend wants somebody who would do a piece of work well — and keep quiet about it — very much."

"Why, now you mention it, I shouldn't mind turning my hand to something, sometime. Something in the sneaking way, where it was pretty sure work and not much more risk than being at home."

"Good," said Fagin, leaning over the table,

after Charlotte had taken the bundle up stairs, "I want you to do a piece of work that needs great care and caution."

"Well, don't yer go shoving me into danger. That don't suit, that don't, not one little bit, I tell yer!"

"There's not the slightest danger in it — not the very smallest. I want you to follow a woman and tell me where she goes, who she sees, and, if possible, what she says — and to bring me back all the information as quickly as you can."

"An old woman?"

"A young one."

"Who is she?"

"One of us. She has found out some new friends, my dear, and I must know who they are."

"I was a regular cunning sneak when I was at school, Fagin, I'm yer man."

"I knew you would be," cried Fagin, elated by the success of his proposal.

"Where is she? Where am I to wait for her? When am I to go?"

"All that, you shall hear from me at the proper time my dear. You keep ready and leave the rest to me."

That night and the next and the next again, Noah Claypole sat ready to turn out at a word from Fagin. Six nights passed, six long weary nights, and on each Fagin came with a disappointed face and said that it was not yet time. On the seventh, a Sunday, he returned and said,

"She goes out tonight. Come with me, quick!"

They left the house stealthily and hurrying through a labyrinth of streets arrived at length before a public house. They entered and Fagin held Noah by his coat behind a curtain. He pointed to a young woman who was looking down sadly at the table.

"Is that her?" asked Noah.

"Yes," said Fagin. "Wait until she turns her face so you can see her plainly."

At that moment, Nancy obligingly turned round.

"I see her now," said Noah, "I should know her among a thousand."

Nancy soon got up and left. Noah exchanged a look with Fagin and darted out. By the light of the street lamp he saw the girl's retreating figure, already at some distance before him. He advanced as near as he dared and kept on the opposite side of the street. Nancy looked

nervously round. She seemed to gather courage as she advanced and began to walk with a firmer step. The spy kept his distance, but never once took his eye off her.

The church clocks chimed three quarters past eleven as two figures emerged on London Bridge. It was a very dark night. A mist hung low over the river. At nearly the centre of the bridge, Nancy stopped. Noah stopped too, and shrinking into one of the recesses which surmount the piers of the bridge, he watched and waited.

The hour had not struck two minutes when a young lady, accompanied by a gentleman, walked up to Nancy.

"Not here," she said hurriedly. "I'm afraid to speak to you here. Down the steps, yonder."

Quickly, Noah went to the spot Nancy had

pointed to and hid.

"Put Monks into my hands," Noah heard the gentleman say, "and leave him to me to deal with."

Noah then heard Nancy tell Mr Brownlow what Monks looked like and where he would find him. "He's tall and strongly made, but not stout. His face is dark, like his hair and eyes. I've only seen him twice and both times he was covered up in a large cloak, but on his throat, when he turns his face, there's . . ."

"A broad red mark, like a burn."

"You know him?" exclaimed Nancy.

"I think I do," said Mr Brownlow. "We shall see. It may not be the same. Now, you have given us the most valuable assistance. What can I do to help you?"

"Nothing, sir," answered the girl, weeping. "You can do nothing to help me. I am past all hope."

"Don't speak thus," pleaded Rose. "There must be something we can do."

"No, nothing! God bless you. Goodnight, goodnight! You must go before someone sees us!"

Mr Brownlow drew his arm through Rose's and gently led her away. As they disappeared Nancy sank to the pavement and sobbed bitter tears. After a while she rose and with feeble and tottering steps climbed the stone stairs to the street above.

Noah remained motionless for some minutes after Nancy had gone, then, peeping out to make sure nobody was about, darted away at his

utmost speed to Fagin's house.

"At last! At last!" muttered Fagin when the boy returned. No sooner had Noah told Fagin what he had seen and heard than a bell rang gently. Fagin crept to the door and presently returned with Bill Sikes.

"Tell me again — once again, just for him to hear," said Fagin, pointing to Sikes as he spoke.

"Tell me what?" asked Sikes.

"About Nancy!" said Fagin, clutching Sikes by the wrist. "You followed her?" he said to Noah.

"Yes."

"To London Bridge?"

"Yes."

"Where she met two people?"

"So she did."

"A gentlemen and a lady who asked her to give up all her pals and to describe Monks, which she did, and to tell which house it was that we meet at and go to, which she did, and what time the people went there, which she did. She did all this. She told it all every word without a threat,

did she not?" screamed Fagin, half mad with fury.

"All right," replied Noah. "That's just what she did!"

"Hell's fire!" cried Sikes, breaking free from Fagin's grip. "Let me go!"

Flinging the old man from him, he rushed from the room.

"Bill, Bill!" cried Fagin. "You won't be too — violent, Bill? Not too violent, Bill, for safety."

Sikes made no reply but, pulling open the door, dashed into the street. Without a pause, without once turning his head, his teeth set tightly, the robber did not relax a muscle until he reached his own door. He opened it softly with a key, strode lightly upstairs and entering his own room, double locked the door and lifting a heavy table against it, drew back the curtain of the bed.

"Get up!" he yelled.

"Bill," replied Nancy. "Why do you look like that at me!"

The robber placed his heavy hand on her mouth.

"Bill, Bill, I — I — won't scream or cry —hear me — tell me what I've done!"

"You know, you she-devil! You were watched tonight. Every word you said was heard."

"Spare my life, for the love of Heaven," cried Nancy, clinging to him in despair.

Sikes struggled, violently, to release his arms.

Freeing one arm, he grasped his pistol and with all his force beat it twice upon the upturned face that almost touched his own. Nancy staggered and fell, nearly blinded with the blood that rained down from a deep gash in her head. Sikes, staggering backward to the wall, seized a heavy club and struck her down with one swift blow.

9 The Pursuit

Twilight was beginning to close in when Mr Brownlow alighted from the hackney-carriage outside his house and knocked softly at the front door. The door being opened, a sturdy man got out of the coach and positioned himself on one side of the steps, while another man, who had been sitting on the box, dismounted too. At a sign from Mr Brownlow, they helped out a third man, and taking him between them, hurried him into the house. This man was Monks.

They walked up the stairs without speaking, with Mr Brownlow leading the way into a back room. "If he gives you any trouble," he said to the two men holding Monks, "drag him into the street and call for the police."

"How dare you kidnap me and bring me here by force!" shouted Monks.

"As I said a moment ago," replied Mr Brownlow, "you are free to go. But if you do I will call the police immediately, and prefer my charges publicly."

Plainly disconcerted, Monks hesitated.

"It is because I was your father's oldest friend," said Mr Brownlow, "that I am moved to treat you gently. I know that your name is not Monks — it is Edward Leeford. I knew your father well and was engaged to marry his sister who died many years ago on the very day we were to be married."

"This is all mighty fine," said Monks, "but what do you want with me?"

"I also know that you have a brother," said Mr Brownlow, "a brother whose name when I spoke it earlier startled you."

"I have no brother. You know I was an only child. Why do you talk to me of a brother?"

"The only child of your father's *first* marriage, it is true," said Mr Brownlow. "But after your parents separated, your father met and fell in love with a beautiful young girl called Agnes Fleming, who died giving birth to their child in a workhouse. Your father, as you know, had already died while on business in Rome.

"Later, many years later, it chanced that a poor boy fell into my care, a boy whom I recognized because of the likeness he bore to a portrait of Agnes your father had left in my care before he went abroad. That boy, as you know, is Oliver Twist."

"I never heard the name before," cried Monks, looking more and more nervous at Mr Brownlow's revelations.

"And I also know that you planned to ensnare Oliver into a life of crime and have him murdered so that you could have all your father's money — money that was left to both you and Oliver."

"You — you — can't prove anything against me," stammered Monks.

"We shall see," returned Mr Brownlow, cooly. "When I lost Oliver I knew that you alone could solve the mystery and as I had heard that you were in the West Indies, I made the voyage. There I learned of your life of crime and that you had left months before for London. And I have

searched to find you ever since. But not until Nancy told me where you might be found did I have a clue as to your whereabouts.''

"And now you do see me,'' said Monks boldly, "what are you going to do about it? You can prove nothing. You can't even prove that Oliver was the son of my father and this Agnes.''

"You know as well as I do that you destroyed the only piece of evidence when you threw the locket bearing her name into the river. Nancy heard you tell Fagin that. Nancy is now dead, brutally murdered, the newspaper says.''

"I — I — know nothing of that . . .''

"Then sign this confession stating what I know to be true, or I will hand you over to the police for robbery and fraud.''

Monks paced up and down, meditating with dark and evil looks on his prospects of evading Mr Brownlow's choice, when Mr Grimwig burst into the room to say that Sikes had been cornered down by the river.

"Go and see what happens, Grimwig, and make sure that they take Fagin too. Now, have

you made up your mind?'' he asked, turning to Monks.

"Yes,'' replied Monks. "If you agree not to tell the police and let me go, I'll sign the confession.''

By the time Mr Grimwig reached the house on the river where Sikes was believed to be hiding, a small crowd had gathered. Some shouted to those who were nearest to set the house on fire, others roared to the police to shoot Sikes dead on sight. There was another roar when the door to the house was at last forced open.

Panic-stricken by the violence of the crowd, and the sound of approaching footsteps, Sikes climbed out on to the roof-top, carrying a rope, with which to lower himself to the ground.

"They have him now,'' cried a man from the crowd. There was another roar.

Sikes set his foot against the stack of chimneys, fastened one end of the rope tightly and firmly round it, and with the other made a strong running noose. At the very instant he brought the loop over his head, before slipping it under his arm-pits, Mr Grimwig saw him and shouted. As if struck by lightning, Sikes suddenly staggered, lost his balance and tumbled over the parapet. The noose was at his neck. With an unearthly screech of terror he plummeted towards the ground. There was a sudden jerk, a convulsion of the limbs and the murderer swung lifeless against the wall.

At two o'clock the following afternoon Fagin was arrested by the police, acting on information given to them by Mr Brownlow. In due course he was tried and sentenced to death. As they brought him from the condemned cell to the gallows he struggled desperately for an instant, then sent up cry upon cry that penetrated even those massive walls.

A great multitude had already assembled as the day dawned. The windows were filled with people, smoking and playing cards to pass the time. The crowd were pushing, quarreling and joking. Everything told of life and animation but one dark cluster of objects in the very centre of all — the black stage, the gallows, the rope and the hideous apparatus of death.

Epilogue

So the fortunes of those who have figured in this tale are nearly closed. With his portion of his father's will Edward Leeford, still calling himself Monks, fled to America, where after a long confinement for fraud, he died in prison.

Noah Claypole was given a free pardon after having testified againt Fagin and found his true vocation as a government informer.

Mr and Mrs Bumble, after having confessed to Mr Brownlow of their part in hiding Oliver's true identity, were deprived of their jobs and reduced to great misery, finally became paupers themselves in that very same workhouse in which they had once inflicted such suffering on so many others.

The Artful Dodger, finally caught in the act of picking a pocket, impressed all at his trial by his arrogance and cleverness: as a result he was given a lengthy prison sentence with which Fagin would have been well pleased.

And as for Oliver, he was adopted by Mr Brownlow and with Mrs Bedwin went to live in the country close to the house where Rose and Mrs Maylie lived. And there they were visited a great many times in the course of the year by Mr Grimwig, whose odd and eccentric manner did not mellow with the years. Thus joined together a little society, whose condition approached as nearly to one of perfect happiness as can ever be known in this changing world.

David Copperfield

Introduction

IN the preface to the 1869 edition of *David Copperfield*, published just before his death, Dickens wrote: "Of all my books, I like this the best. It will be easily believed that I am a fond parent to every child of my fancy, and that no-one can ever love that family as dearly as I love them. But, like many fond parents, I have in my heart of hearts a favourite child. And his name is *David Copperfield*."

Dickens started the book in London in February 1849 and finished it at Broadstairs, on the Kent coast, in October 1850. Like most of his novels it was published as a "part-work", monthly instalments of 32 pages with two engraved illustrations.

Parts of *David Copperfield* clearly reflect parts of Dickens' own life. In fact he originally intended to write his life story and publish it after his death, but he soon abandoned the idea and put many of his experiences and feelings into the novel instead.

John Dickens, his father, is the obvious inspiration for Mr Micawber; he had all Mr Micawber's virtues — charm, generosity, eloquence, optimism — and the same hopeless irresponsibility with money. When his father was sent to prison for debt the 12-year-old Charles went to work at a "blacking" (ink) factory near the River Thames, a business managed by a friend of the Dickens family. He earned six shillings (the cost of an ice-cream in today's money) for 68 hours' work a week. Though he was earning money badly needed by his family, Charles felt humiliated and abandoned.

Many other events in Dickens' life are present in *David Copperfield*. David's miserable time at Salem House school is an echo of Dickens' short attendance at Wellington House Academy, the school his father sent him to after his job at the factory, and Mr Creakle is accurately based on Dickens' own headmaster, William Jones. Like Dickens, David begins his literary career as a reporter and writer of short stories, and soon becomes a famous novelist; like Dickens, he produces a houseful of children whom he adores.

Why is *David Copperfield* still read with such delight today? First of all, it is simply a great story — romantic, but also realistic and believable. Second, it excites all our emotions, from rib-tickling laughter to tears of pity. Third, it is almost impossible not to like David, to feel for him and wish him well. Most of his qualities — modesty, frankness, trustworthiness, honesty, goodwill — are ones we admire, and his frailties are understandable and endearing. And last, of course, it contains a cast of wonderful, larger-than-life characters: Peggotty, Mr Micawber, Uriah Heep, Betsey Trotwood, and a host of others. Their names will last as long as Dickens' own.

1 Early Days

To begin my story with the beginning of my life, I record that I was born (or so I have been informed and believe) on a Friday in March, at twelve o'clock at night. This event took place at my mother's house near the village of Blunderstone, in the county of Suffolk.

My father's eyes had been closed on the light of this world six months when mine opened on it — a fact which helps to account for the sudden appearance of a strange visitor on the very day of my own arrival.

This bold lady, having first startled my poor mother by looking in at the window, then entered the house and approached her as she sat by the fire.

"Mrs David Copperfield, I think?" she asked.

"Yes," replied my mother, faintly.

"You have heard, I dare say, of Miss Betsey Trotwood, aunt of your late husband? Well, now you see her!"

Before she could muster a word in reply, my mother burst into tears.

"Oh come, come! Don't do that!" said Miss Trotwood, giving her a handkerchief. "Why bless my heart, look at you — you're only a child, and here you are with child yourself. Now, what's the matter, my dear?"

"I'm — I'm all in a tremble. I don't know what will happen. I'll die, I'm sure I'll die!"

"That, my child, is absolute nonsense! What you need is a good strong cup of tea. Now, what do you call your girl?"

"I don't know that it will be a girl."

"No, no. I don't mean the baby. I mean what do you call your servant girl?"

"Oh! Peggotty."

"Peggotty! How very extraordinary!"

"Her Christian name is Clara," explained my mother patiently. "But that's the same as mine, so I call her by her surname to avoid confusion."

"I see," said Miss Trotwood, walking to the door. "Peggotty! We need some tea! Don't dawdle now!"

She resumed her seat by the fire, still wearing her bonnet. "I have no doubt that this baby of yours will be a girl," she continued. "Now, from the moment of the birth this girl —"

"Perhaps boy."

"Don't contradict me, child! I intend to be your daughter's godmother, and I beg you to call her Betsey Trotwood Copperfield. There will be no mistakes in life with *this* Betsey Trotwood. There must be no trifling with *her* affections, poor dear. *She* must be well brought up and well guarded. And I must make that my care!"

Before my mother could contest this suggestion she collapsed in her chair, just as Peggotty came in with a tray. "It's the doctor you need, ma'am," she said firmly, "not a cup of tea!"

"Well don't just stand there, Peggotty!" cried Miss Trotwood. "Be off and fetch the man. Quickly!"

While all around her busied themselves with carrying my mother upstairs and preparing for the great happening, Miss Trotwood stopped up her ears with cotton-wool and sat down by the fire, with her embroidery as company. And she was still there several hours later when Peggotty entered the room carrying the new-born child in her ample arms.

"Would you like to see the baby, Miss Trotwood? He's a strong little thing, with a pair of lungs like the wind at sea."

The visitor rose from her chair. "How is she?"

"Oh, she's comfortable, ma'am. The doctor says she's as comfortable as a young mother can expect to be under these melancholy domestic circumstances."

"Peggotty, you would appear to have a mind every bit as wondrous as your name. I meant the baby. How is she?"

"My name seems no less wondrous than your understandin', ma'am. The baby is a boy. We've called him David, after his father — David Copperfield."

I am told that my great aunt said not a word,

but picked up her basket, put on her coat and walked out into the night. She vanished like a discontented fairy — and never returned.

Looking back into my infancy, the first objects I can remember as standing out by themselves from a confusion of things are my mother, with her pretty hair and youthful shape, and Peggotty, with hardly any shape at all. I remember, too, that we were both a little afraid of Peggotty, and submitted ourselves in most matters to her direction. And I remember that I was very happy.

Late one summer evening, when I was eight or so, I was gazing out of the window on to the garden when I saw my mother bidding goodbye

to a tall, dark gentleman. His name was Mr Murdstone, and he had walked home with us from church on several Sundays. When my mother came into the room, she looked even more beautiful than usual.

"I hope you had a pleasant evenin', ma'am," inquired Peggotty, rather coolly.

"Oh yes, thank you, Peggotty," replied my mother, taking off her bonnet in front of the mirror. "I had a very pleasant evening indeed!"

"A stranger or so makes an agreeable change," suggested Peggotty.

"You don't approve of my going out, do you, Peggotty? But tell me, what should I do? Shave my head and hide my face, or disfigure myself with a burn?"

"Mr Copperfield wouldn't have liked such a one as this. That I say and that I swear."

"Oh stop, Peggotty! Stop!" cried my mother, bursting into tears. "You'll upset David!"

There was an awkward silence during which everyone regretted what had been said.

"Perhaps what he needs is a holiday by the sea," said Peggotty finally. "Would you like to go along and stay with my brother and his family at Yarmouth, Davy?"

"Is your brother an agreeable man?" I asked.

"Oh, what an agreeable man he is!" cried Peggotty, holding up her hands. "Then there's the sea and the boats and the beach and my nephew Ham and little Em'ly —"

"I'd love to go," I said, and the arrangement was sealed with hugs and kisses.

The day soon arrived for our trip to Yarmouth, which would be by horse and cart. The carrier, whose name was Barkis — a man of remarkably few words — owned what must have been the slowest horse in the world, so the journey took most of the day, and we were thankful for Peggotty's fine pies.

When we eventually arrived on the edge of Yarmouth we were met by Peggotty's nephew. "There's my Ham," she cried, "growed out of all knowin'."

Peggotty was right, for this 'boy' she had described to me was now a huge strong fellow of six feet, and broad in proportion. He took our bags and put me on his back to guide us along the beach.

Suddenly he stopped. "Yon's our house, Mas'r Davy!" he said, putting me down.

I looked in all directions, as far as I could see, but I could make out no house. There was an upturned boat not far away, high and dry off the ground, with a smoking iron funnel for a chimney; but nothing else in the way of habitation was visible to me. "That's it?" I asked. "That ship-looking thing?" They both said it was, and I could not have been more charmed by the idea of living in it had it been Aladdin's palace.

From this unusual home appeared a bearded, pipe-smoking fisherman and, behind him at the door, a girl not much older than myself.

"Davy, this is my brother," said Peggotty, "and that there's little Em'ly."

"We're glad to see you, sir," said Mr Peggotty with a broad smile. "You'll find us rough but you'll find us ready. And I hope you'll stay as long as you've a mind to."

The girl darted into the house. "She's a shy one, that little Em'ly," laughed Mr Peggotty. "God bless her. Now come on, young Davy, I'll show you your room."

After tea, when the door was shut and all was made snug, this place seemed to me the most enchanting retreat the imagination could conceive. Emily had overcome her shyness and sat next to me by the fire; later, when Peggotty tucked me up in bed, she told me that Emily was an orphan whom Mr Peggotty had adopted as his very own — as he had done with Ham.

The next morning I was up early and soon out on the beach with Emily, picking up stones.

"You're quite a sailor, I expect?" I said.

"No," replied Emily. "I'm afraid of the sea."

"Afraid!" I said, looking out across the water. "I'm not!"

"But it's cruel. It's very cruel, the sea. I've seen it tear a boat as big as our house to pieces."

"I hope it wasn't the boat that —"

"That my father was drownded in? No, not that one. I never see that boat."

"Nor him?"

Emily shook her pretty head. "Not to remember, anyhow."

"I never saw my father, either."

"Your father was a gentleman — mine was a fisherman. And so's my uncle."

"He seems a very good man, Mr Peggotty."

"Good? If I was ever to be a lady I'd give him a sky-blue coat with diamond buttons and a pipe made out of silver."

"You'd like to be a lady, then?"

"Oh yes. I'd like it more than anything."

We walked a long way and loaded ourselves up with all kinds of curious things before turning back towards Mr Peggotty's home. "Look at you two," he said as we went in for breakfast. "Just like a pair of young thrushes!"

The blissful days at Yarmouth flew by and soon Mr Barkis, who lived not far away, arrived with his cart and trusty steed. It broke my heart to leave Emily, but Mr Peggotty said I would be welcome at any time — and Peggotty assured me as we set off for Blunderstone that her brother was a man of his word.

After that, however, she went strangely silent, and as we neared our village I saw a tear or two trickle down her plump cheek.

"Why, Peggotty, what is it?"

"Wait, Davy — wait till we get inside."

Peggotty took me into the kitchen and closed the door behind us.

"What is it, Peggotty? What's the matter?"

"I should have told you afore now," she said quietly, holding my hand, "but, well, you were so busy and so happy I couldn't exactly bring my mind to it. Now what do you think, Davy — you've got a father! Come and see him."

"I don't want to see him!"

"And your mother?" said Peggotty.

My heart was pounding. She led me into the parlour and went back to the kitchen. On one side of the fire sat my mother; on the other stood Mr Murdstone. My mother got up to come to me, but suddenly stopped.

"Now Clara, control yourself!" snapped Mr Murdstone. "Always control yourself!"

He walked towards me and held out his hand. "Davy boy, how do you do?"

I shook his hand but could say nothing. I went and kissed my mother, but I could not look at her — and I could not look at him.

I left the room and ran into the kitchen. "Oh, Peggotty, I don't like him. I don't want a father, especially not Mr Murdstone!"

"I knew it would be hard for you, Davy. That's why I took you to the seaside. It's going to be hard for me too, but we'll just have to make the best of it, won't we?"

"Is he here to stay?" I asked, already knowing the dreadful answer.

"Yes, Davy, he is — and his sister arrives tomorrow evening!"

I crept upstairs and found that my dear bedroom, like everything in the house, had been changed. My mother came up to see me in my new room, but Mr Murdstone soon followed and sent her down, telling her that she must compose herself and be firm with me from then on.

2 I Am Sent to School

I could see that Mr Murdstone was fond of my mother, but I'm afraid I liked him none the better for that. I longed for a word of encouragement or even explanation, of welcome home, of reassurance that it *was* home. It may at least have made me respect him rather than just hate him.

The following evening his sister arrived, and Peggotty led me into the hall to meet her. A miserable looking lady she was, dark and unsmiling like her brother, and as far as I could make out she had come to stay for good; indeed within hours she was running the entire household.

As the days passed, a suffocating gloom settled on our house, with never a smile to brighten any day, and with Sundays even more of a trial than the rest. My only consolation were the storybooks left by my father, and I spent hour after hour buried in *Robinson Crusoe, The Arabian Nights* and many other tales of adventure in my room.

Firmness was the one virtue on which both Mr and Miss Murdstone insisted. An iron discipline reigned, with my mother as much a

subject as myself. There was occasional talk about my going to boarding-school, but in the meantime I continued my lessons at home.

I was scrutinized by all three adults during these lessons, and they were the greatest burden of my dreary life. The influence of the Murdstones was like the cruel fascination of two snakes on a wretched bird.

One evening Mr Murdstone held in his hand a cane, which he now and again swished to impress me.

"Now, David," he said, putting the cane on the table, "you must be far more careful today than usual with your answers."

I was indeed extremely careful, but I still faltered several times. Suddenly Mr Murdstone stood up. "You must and *will* learn your lessons off by heart, boy. Do you understand?"

"But Mr Murdstone, sir! I find it difficult to do my work with you and Miss Murdstone so close by me."

"I will not tolerate such impudence, boy!" he shouted, flexing the cane with his hands. "You and I will go upstairs!"

"Please, Edward. No!" pleaded my mother.

"Are you a *perfect* fool, Clara," interrupted Miss Murdstone. "You are too soft with the boy. He needs discipline — and discipline he shall have!"

Mr Murdstone walked me up to my room slowly and gravely, like an executioner leading his doomed prisoner, and once there gripped my head under his arm. But I wriggled free for a moment, pleading with him not to beat me.

It was only a moment, for he then grabbed my collar and cut me heavily with the cane, and in the same instant I clenched the hand that held me between my teeth, and bit it through. Even now, it sets my teeth on edge to think of it.

He beat me then, as though he would have beaten me to death. But above all our noise I still heard the running on the stairs — my mother crying out — and Peggotty. Then he was gone, and the door locked. And I was lying, hot and sore and torn, on the floor.

When I became quiet I lay listening for a while, but there was not a sound. My cuts were sore and stiff, and made me ache if I tried to move, but they were nothing to the guilt I felt.

Miss Murdstone appeared next morning before I was out of bed and told me I was free to walk in the garden for half an hour, and no longer. I did so, with some difficulty that first day, and did so every morning of my imprisonment, which lasted five days; and I saw no-one except that awesome creature during that time.

The length of those five tormented days I cannot convey to anyone; they occupy the place of years in my memory. Every detail of that room, every sound that reached me from the world outside it, are etched on my mind.

On the last evening of my punishment, I suddenly heard my own name, spoken in a whisper on the other side of the door.

"Is that you, Peggotty?"

"Yes, my own precious Davy. But be as soft as a mouse, or the cat will hear us!"

"How's mama, Peggotty? Is she angry with me?"

"No, not very."

"What's going to be done with me?"

"School, Davy. Near London. Tomorrow."

"Shall I see mama?"

"Yes, in the mornin'. 'Night, darlin' boy."

"Goodnight, Peggotty — and thank you!"

In the morning, at breakfast, I ran into my mother's arms and begged her to forgive me.

"Oh, Davy!" she said. "That you could hurt anyone I love! Try to be better, pray to be better. I forgive you, but I'm so grieved that you should have such bad passions in your heart."

Mr Barkis was to take me to Yarmouth, where next day I would board the coach to London. There, at the ticket office, I would be met by a master and escorted to the school, which was across the river in the district of Blackheath.

My mother came out to see me off on a fine summer's day, with Miss Murdstone hovering by her side. "Goodbye, my child," she said softly. "You are going for your own good. You will come home in the holidays and be a better boy. God bless you, my darling!"

The lazy horse had gone about half a mile — and I had almost stopped crying — when Mr Barkis suddenly pulled him up as Peggotty dashed out from a hedge.

"Here, Davy," she said, handing me a paper bag. "I've baked some cakes for your journey — and here's a purse with seven shillings in it. From your mother, with her love." And with that she feel into deep sobs and turned to walk quickly back to the house.

After some miles I took out Peggotty's bag and offered Mr Barkis one of her cakes, which he consumed in one gulp.

"Did she make that?" he inquired.

I told him that Peggotty did all our cooking.

"Do she though!" said Mr Barkis, stirring in his seat and turning his gaze on me. "No sweethearts, I believe? No person walks with her?"

I said I didn't think that Peggotty had ever had a sweetheart.

"Didn't she, though!" said Mr Barkis. "Well, I'll tell you what. If you was writin' to her, p'raps you'd recollect to say that Barkis is willin'."

"That Barkis is willing," I repeated. "Is that all the message?"

"Aye, that's all. You just tell her that. Barkis is willin'."

On my arrival at Salem House, for that was the name of my school, I was sent to wait outside the study of the headmaster, one Mr Creakle. The place was almost deserted, and I could not help but wonder, as I sat trying to read my book, why I could neither see nor hear any other boys.

The door opened and there stood before me a stout, bald man whose fiery eyes seemed to be sunk deep in his head. He pointed for me to enter, then banged the door shut behind him.

"So you're Copperfield, eh?"

"Yes, sir," I replied, quite quaking with fear.

"I have the pleasure of knowing your step-father," said Mr Creakle, taking me by the ear, "and a worthy man he is. I know him and he knows me. Do you know me, boy, eh?"

"Not yet, sir," I said, flinching with pain.

"Not yet. But you soon will, eh?"

"I hope so, sir."

"You're very smart, Copperfield, very smart," said Mr Creakle, finally letting go of my ear, "for a boy who bites!" He took a sheet of card from his desk and held it up before me:

"What does this say, boy, eh?"

"It says 'I bite', sir."

"You'll wear this on your back, boy, until I say that you can take it off!"

"Oh, please, sir, must I?"

Mr Creakle raised his cane above his head. "When I say I'll do a thing, boy, I do it," he shouted, bringing the cane crashing down on the desk, "and when I say I'll have a thing done, I will have it done! Turn around, boy!"

He fixed the card to my jacket and ordered me out of his study.

It transpired that the other boys were not due back for the half-year term until the next day. I was dreading their making fun of me, so it was a happy circumstance for me that it was Tommy Traddles, a plump, friendly character, who was the first to return. He found it very amusing, and used the card as a form of introduction to the others with the words, "Look here, here's a game!" Some boys mocked me, saying "Lie down, sir!" and calling me dogs' names, but on the whole it was better than I had expected.

Traddles' last introduction was to J. Steer-forth. I was taken before this boy, who was said to be a great scholar and athlete, and was at least half-a-dozen years my senior, as if before a magistrate.

"What money have you got, Copperfield?"

I told him seven shillings.

"You had better give it to me to take care of," he said. "At least, you can if you like. You needn't if you don't want to."

I opened my purse into his hand.

"Do you want to spend anything now?"

"No thank you, sir."

"Perhaps you'd like to spend a shilling or so on a bottle of redcurrant wine for later, up in the dormitory," suggested Steerforth. "You belong to my dormitory, I believe."

I said yes, I should like that.

"Good. I dare say you'll be glad to spend another shilling or so on almond cake, and another shilling or so on biscuits, and another on fruit, eh?"

I said I would like that, too.

"I can go out when I like," said Steerforth, "so I'll smuggle the stuff in for you." And with that he pocketed the seven coins and walked away.

I was a little worried, I confess, about handing over my mother's present so readily, but Traddles took me by the arm. "Don't worry, Copperfield," he said quietly. "Steerforth's not a bully. You'll see."

Indeed I did, for that evening when we went to bed there was a whole seven shillings' worth laid out on my bed.

"There you are, young Copperfield, and a right royal spread you've got."

We did the feast proud, and continued talking in whispered tones until well past the time to go to sleep.

"Goodnight, young Copperfield," said Steerforth. "I'll take good care of you."

"You're very kind," I replied. "Goodnight."

It was Steerforth's clever ploy that, after a few days, had my card removed. He informed Mr Creakle that it was a nuisance when masters wished to hit me with their canes as they passed,

and it was then taken off, to my great relief.

There was only one event in this half-year, outside the daily life of the school, which still survives in my mind: a visit — my only one — of some dear acquaintances. I was called out from

the class one late summer afternoon and there, in the courtyard, stood Mr Peggotty and Ham.

I could not stop myself bursting into tears at the sight of them, and felt a little ashamed.

"Cheer up, Mas'r Davy!" said Ham. "Why, how you've growed!"

"Ain't he growed!" echoed Mr Peggotty.

"We brought you some victuals, Mas'r Davy," said Ham, bending over a fisherman's basket; and he produced a lobster, crabs and a great bag of shrimps.

"They're all boiled ready," explained Mr Peggotty. "We was bringin' down a lug to Gravesend so we thought we'd take the liberty of comin' over to pay a visit."

"Oh, I'm so glad you did, and thank you. Tell me, Mr Peggotty, how's dear Emily?"

"She's uncommon well, Davy," he replied, "uncommon well. And she's getting to be somethin' of a woman, now."

Ham beamed with delight at the very mention of her name. "Her learnin', too, Mas'r Davy."

"And writin'!" added Mr Peggotty. "So large it is, you might see it anywheres."

I was telling them about the school — and trying to conceal its unpleasant aspects — when Steerforth walked across the courtyard towards us, carrying a cricket bat.

"What are you doing out here, young Copperfield?" he asked.

"Steerforth, these are two Yarmouth boatmen who are relations of my nurse, Peggotty. They've come over from Gravesend to see me."

Steerforth was charming and amusing — he had an ability to put anyone at their ease in a moment that I have not yet seen rivalled by any person — and by the time of his departure a few minutes later was being invited up to Yarmouth to view their strange home and go sailing with Mr Peggotty upon the sea.

3 Tragedy and Neglect

Apart from the delight I gave to the whole dormitory by telling the stories I had learned from my books, I remember little of what happened at school in my second term until my birthday — an anniversary that turned out to be the most memorable of my life.

After breakfast I was told I had a visitor and there, in the courtyard, stood Peggotty.

"Peggotty!" I cried. "What a lovely surprise!"

"I wish it were, Davy," she replied solemnly, "I only wish it were. But I'm afraid I've got bad news for you."

"Mama — is she all right?"

"No, Davy, she's not. Your mother has passed on."

"Mother, dead? Oh no, no!"

"There, there, my darlin' boy. She was always a frail creature, never very strong. And now she's gone."

"What — what will become of me, Peggotty?"

"First, you'll come home with me for the funeral, Davy. Then it'll be up to Mr Murdstone to decide what's to be done for the best."

I burst into uncontrollable sobs — whether at the death of my mother or the prospect of the Murdstones in sole control of me, I cannot say.

"There now, Davy," said Peggotty, holding me close to her. "We must both be very brave."

Mr Murdstone took no heed of me when I arrived home, and he was considerably distressed. Not so his sister; she derived a gruesome pleasure in displaying her firmness and self-control and strength of mind in such circumstances, and I loathed her for it.

The first act of business Miss Murdstone performed when the funeral was over, and light was freely admitted into the house, was to give Peggotty two weeks' notice to quit.

"What are you going to do, Peggotty?"

"I'll try to find a position close by so that I can be near to you, Davy, but if I can't then I shall go to my brother's — just till I've had time to look about me for suitable employment in Yarmouth."

But Peggotty's quest round Blunderstone was unsuccessful; the day for her departure dawned all too soon, and Mr Barkis arrived with his faithful horse outside the garden gate.

"Excuse me, miss," said Mr Barkis, after loading up the cart. "I asked this young gentleman 'ere on more than one occasion to tell you that Barkis is willin'. And now I'm tellin' you that Barkis is *still* willin'."

If it had not been for the natural redness of Peggotty's complexion, I would have sworn she blushed. "I'm sure I don't know what you're talking about," she replied airily. "Now Davy, I want you to know that you will always be my darlin' boy. I'll come and see you when I can."

"Thank you, Peggotty."

"I'm ready, Mr Barkis," she said firmly, getting into the cart. "And you keep your eyes fixed on that road!"

Peggotty had boldly suggested that since it appeared I was not to return to school, I should go with her for a holiday at Yarmouth. Nothing would have been a greater thrill for me in those trying times.

"The boy will be idle there," retorted Miss Murdstone, "and idleness is the root of all evil; though my brother would appreciate the quiet during his period of suffering more than I can say."

Heaven only knows I was idle enough at Blunderstone. The restraints that used to hold me were now lifted, though I was still not permitted to mix with others of my own age.

I was not ill-treated; I was not beaten or starved. But the wrong that was done to me was unrelenting. Day after day, week after week, month after month, it was as if I just did not exist. I simply fell into a state of neglect.

The only light in this bleak picture came from the visits, every two or three weeks, of dear Peggotty. On one such day, and much to my surprise, she suddenly announced that she was now married.

"That's wonderful!" I cried. "May I ask to whom?"

"To Barkis, of course!" she replied, a little puzzled at my inquiry. "I'll have him as long as he behaves."

We both laughed as she related how, at her brother's boathouse, Barkis had arrived every evening with silly little gifts for her, until she finally agreed to his request; and how they slipped away and were married in a church near Barkis' house, with no-one suspecting any such event until it had been completed.

One evening, after the best part of a year of this weary existence with my guardians, the master of the house announced that he had something of importance to say to me.

"Education is costly, David," he began, his

mean-faced sister standing by his side. "But even if it were not, I am of the firm opinion that it would be no advantage to return you to that school — or to any other. To the young this is a world for action, not for moping in —"

"As you do!" added his sister, looking at me.

"Leave this to me, please, Jane. What is before you is a fight with the world, and the sooner you begin it, the better. I have arranged for you to work at the firm of Murdstone and Grinby, in which I have a small interest, in London. You will earn enough for yourself to live on, with a little more for pocket-money. Your lodgings and washing will be paid for by me."

"You are provided for," observed his sister smugly, "and will be pleased to do your duty."

I have no recollection of whether I was pleased at this turn of events or not, but the very next day I left for London and the morning after that I was put to work in a warehouse cellar down by the river at Blackfriars.

Murdstone and Grinby were wine merchants and my job consisted of examining the returned bottles against the light for flaws and cracks and, if they were not rejected, to wash, rinse, label and re-cork or re-seal them, and put the finished items into cases. For this labour, from eight in the morning until eight at night, I was to be paid the princely sum of six shillings a week.

I was reflecting on the sadness of my plight that first morning when, around midday, there appeared on the steps to the cellar a stoutish, middle-aged person in a red coat, tight brown trousers and black shoes. He boasted an imposing shirt collar and a large top hat.

"Master Copperfield, I presume!" he said, taking off the hat and revealing a head with no more hair upon it than there is upon an egg. "I trust I find you well, sir?"

I said I was, and hoped that he was.

"Yes, quite so. My name is Micawber — Wilkins Micawber. I have been requested by Mr Murdstone to receive you as a lodger, and as I understand that your knowledge of London is

not yet extensive, I feel it my duty to present myself in this subterranean workplace at the appropriate time and escort you to my home."

I thanked him heartily for his consideration and told him that I finished at eight o'clock.

He appeared at the appointed time and guided me through the murky streets to his house off the City Road, providing me with such information that I should find my way back in the morning.

Once inside this house — which struck me as like its occupant, shabby but making all the show it could — I was introduced to Mrs Micawber, a thin and faded lady, and to their four small children.

"I never thought that I should find it necessary to take in a lodger," she said when Mr Micawber had disappeared on one of his frequent excursions, "but Mr Micawber being in such dire financial difficulties, all private feelings must be put aside. For all that, Master Copperfield, you are most welcome."

In this house, watching Mr and Mrs Micawber wrestle with their monetary problems and, in vain, to stave off their creditors, I spent most of my precious leisure time. I had little choice, since after paying for my own food there was barely anything left of my wages. When I did decide on a solitary treat, and visited a public house, I was often refused custom because I was so young.

In my forlorn state I became quite attached to the Micawbers and used to walk about, busy with Mrs Micawber's calculations for solving the problems and heavy with the weight of Mr Micawber's debts. On a Saturday night, which was my special treat (I went home early, with six shillings in my pocket), Mrs Micawber would make heart-rending confessions to me. And it would be nothing for Mr Micawber to sob violently at his plight at the start of such an evening, and then be singing his head off with happiness at the end of it. Thus a curious equality of friendship sprung up between us, despite the great disparity in our years.

One summer's day, the very next after Mrs Micawber had confided in me that her husband's difficulties were rapidly coming to a crisis, the said gentleman appeared at my place of work.

"Would you care for some lunch, Master Copperfield?" he asked, handing me a little bundle.

"Thank you, Mr Micawber. Would you like some?"

"Alas, Copperfield, there is no time. The miserable wretch you see before is this very moment the object of much wrath from his creditors. He must flee, Copperfield, flee into the night — or day, as the case may be."

"Do you mean you're leaving London?"

"I am, and I thank you for being a model lodger. Permit me, Copperfield, to leave you two pieces of advice. The first is this: never do tomorrow what you can do today. Procrastination is the thief of time. Collar him! And the second piece of advice is this: annual income twenty pounds, annual expenditure nineteen pounds nineteen and six, result — happiness; annual income twenty pounds, annual expenditure twenty pounds ought and six, result — misery!"

"Is there anything I can do to assist you?"

"Bless you, but no! I trust that we shall meet again. Farewell, my young friend!"

"Goodbye, Mr Micawber, and good luck!"

I had grown so accustomed to the Micawbers, and had been so intimate with them in their distresses, and was so utterly friendless without them, that the prospect of being moved to new and unknown lodgings filled me with panic.

I knew quite well that there could be no escape unless I ordered it myself, and there and then I resolved to run away — to go, by some means or other, down to Dover, to the only relation I had in the world, and tell my story to my great aunt, Miss Betsey Trotwood.

4 A New Life

My journey to Dover was hazardous and long, and only once did I enjoy some respite from walking, when a carrier allowed me to lie on the load in his cart for some six miles or so. Having slept in haystacks and secluded barns, coming within a whisker of danger from other travellers on more than one occasion, I arrived in Dover on the fourth day. It was some hours before I found my aunt's house on the outskirts of the town, by which time I was very nearly on the point of exhaustion.

The first person I saw was a bespectacled gentleman gazing out at me from an upstairs window; but before I had time even to call out to him there appeared another figure through the front door. Immediately I knew her to be Miss Betsey, for she came stalking out of her house exactly as my mother had so often described her stalking into ours at Blunderstone.

"Go away!" she shouted, waving her arms about in the air. "No boys here! Go away!"

"If you please, ma'am — I mean aunt."

"Eh?" she exclaimed, in a tone of amazement I have never heard approached, before or since.

"If you please, aunt, I'm your nephew."

"Oh, Lord!" said my aunt, and she staggered

back to sit down on the garden seat.

"I'm David Copperfield, of Blunderstone, in Suffolk — where you came on the very day I was born, and saw my dear mama. I have been very unhappy since she died. I have been slighted, and taught nothing, and put to work not fit for me. It made me run away to you. I've walked almost all the way here from London, and not slept in a bed since I started the journey —"

Here I broke into a passion of crying, fell down on my knees, and put my aching head on Miss Betsey's lap.

My aunt called up to the gentleman at the window to come down and assist her. "Mr Dick," she said as he approached, "you have heard me mention my nephew, David Copperfield? Now don't pretend not to have a memory, because you and I both know better."

"David Copperfield? *David* Copperfield? Oh yes, to be sure. David. Yes, certainly."

"Well, this is his boy. And he has run away. His sister, Betsey Trotwood, never would have run away, of course, had she been born. But the question is, Mr Dick, what shall I do with him?"

"What shall you do with him?" said Mr Dick, scratching his head. "Why, if I were you, I should — I should — wash him!"

"Of course!" said my aunt. "Oh, you're as sharp as a blade, Mr Dick. That's exactly what we'll do with this boy!"

The bath was a great comfort, and when I was

finished they covered me in a shirt and a pair of trousers belonging to Mr Dick, and put two great shawls around me. What sort of bundle I looked like I don't know, but I was a very hot one, and feeling faint and drowsy, I soon lay down on the sofa and fell fast asleep.

Shortly after I woke we had dinner — never has a meal tasted so sweet — and I told my story in as much detail as I could remember. I was also deeply anxious to know what was to become of me, but I thought it best to avoid such questions so soon after my unexpected appearance.

The next day, at breakfast, I plucked up courage to ask my aunt what she intended to do with me.

"I have written to your stepfather about the subject of your arrival —"

"You're not going to give me up to him?"

"I can't say, I'm sure," replied my aunt. "We shall wait and see."

My spirits sank under these words, and I spent the days waiting for news from Mr Murdstone in a constant state of trepidation. The worry was punctuated, however, by some wonderful hours sharing Mr Dick's passion for flying his kite from the cliffs.

After coming inside from one such sunny afternoon, Miss Betsey asked me what I made of her strange companion.

"I — I think he's very nice," I replied.

"Come now! Your sister Betsey Trotwood would have told what she thought of anyone, straight out. Be as like your sister as you can, and speak out!"

"Is he — is he at all out of his mind, then?"

"Not a morsel! He has been called mad, but if he was I should not have enjoyed the company of his society these past ten years. Mr Dick is a sort of distant relation of mine, but I need not enter into that. If it had not been for my intervention, his brother would have shut him up in an asylum for life. That's all."

This admission increased my growing affection for my aunt — a feeling further enhanced by her attitude on the arrival of Mr and Miss Murdstone the following morning. First, she insisted that I be present throughout the interview; then she gave her visitors a round ticking off for allowing Miss Murdstone's horse to trample on the edge of her lawn; and finally she asked for Mr Dick to come down from his room and introduced him as an old and intimate friend on whose judgment she relied entirely.

Mr Murdstone was the first to broach the subject of their visit. "Miss Trotwood, this unhappy boy who has run away from his friends and his occupation —"

"And whose appearance is quite disgraceful!" interposed his sister.

"Jane, have the goodness not to interrupt when I'm —"

"I'm sorry if his appearance does not agree with you," interrupted my aunt. "Mr Dick was kind enough to relinquish part of his wardrobe to clothe the boy."

"It is not his appearance that concerns me, Miss Trotwood, but his character. This boy has been the cause of much trouble. He has a sullen, rebellious spirit and a violent temper. Both my sister and I have tried to correct his vices, but without success."

"If he had been your own boy, would you have beaten him and sent him off to work in London at such a tender age?" asked my aunt.

"If he had been my brother's own boy," returned Miss Murdstone, striking in, "then his character would, I trust, have been altogether different."

"What have you to say next, eh?" asked my aunt.

"Merely this, Miss Trotwood. I am here to take David back, to dispose of him as I think right. You may have some notion of abetting him in his running away, but I must caution you that if you abet him now, you do so for good and

always. I cannot be trifled with."

"I think I have heard quite enough," said my aunt firmly, rising from her chair. "Mr Dick, what shall I do with this child?"

Mr Dick hesitated for a moment and looked round at me before his face lit up. "Have him measured for a suit of clothes immediately!"

"Mr Dick, give me your hand!" said my aunt triumphantly. "Your common sense is invaluable." She pulled me towards her and said to Mr Murdstone, "You can go when you please. I'll take my chance with the boy. If he is all you say he is, then I can do as much for him as you. But I don't believe a single word of it!"

"Miss Trotwood!" cried Mr Murdstone. "If you were a gentleman —"

"Good day, sir, and goodbye!" said Aunt Betsey. "And good day to you, too, ma'am! Let me see you ride a horse over my green again and as sure as you have a head upon your shoulders, I'll knock your bonnet off and tread upon it!"

The Murdstones left without another word, and my aunt, still with a defiant face, turned to her companion. "You will consider yourself guardian, jointly with me, of this child, Mr Dick?"

"I shall be delighted to be the guardian of such a bright young man! Yes, to be sure — I shall be delighted!"

"Very good," said my aunt with a sigh, "then that's all settled."

I was so happy I clasped both my hands round my aunt's neck and kissed her many times. Then I shook hands with Mr Dick and thanked him over and over again, and he hailed this conclusion to the proceedings with repeated bursts of laughter.

Thus I began my new life and I felt, for many days, like one in a dream. The two clearest things in my mind were that a remoteness had come on the old Blunderstone, which seemed to lie in a distant haze; and that a curtain had fallen on my life at Murdstone and Grinby.

Mr Dick and I soon became the best of friends, and very often went out together to fly his huge kite. Nor did I lose any favour with my aunt, and in the course of a few weeks she took to me so kindly that I was encouraged to feel that I may one day enjoy equal rank in her affections with my fictitous sister, Betsey Trotwood.

"David," she said one evening, when the backgammon board was placed as usual for

herself and Mr Dick, "we must not forget your education. Would you like to go to school at Canterbury?"

I replied that, since it was so near to her, I would like it very much.

"Good. Then would you like to go the day after tomorrow?"

I said I would love to, and so all was made ready.

As we set out, my aunt told me that we were going first to the office of a Mr Wickfield, an old

81

friend of hers, a lawyer and a steward of the estates of a rich gentleman of the county. When we knocked at the door of his office it was opened by a skeletal-looking young man dressed in legal black.

"Uriah Heep, is Mr Wickfield at home?"

"Yes, ma'am, he is," replied Uriah Heep. "If you'll please to walk in there." And he pointed with his bony hand to another door.

"Well, Miss Trotwood, what a pleasant surprise," said a handsome, well-dressed gentleman. "And what wind blows you here. Not an ill wind, I trust?"

"No, Mr Wickfield. I wish you to draw up adoption papers for my nephew David here, or rather my grand-nephew, and want your advice on a school in Canterbury where he may be thoroughly well taught — and well treated."

"Well, the best school in the district has no room for boarders just now. But I'll tell you what we can do."

"What is that?" inquired my aunt.

"Leave your nephew here, for the present. If it doesn't turn out for the best, there will be time to find another place. We won't be hard about terms, but you shall pay if you will."

"I am very much obliged to you," said my aunt, "and so is he, I see."

"Then I will fetch my little housekeeper," said Mr Wickfield.

He returned with a girl of about my own age. Although her face was quite bright and happy, there was a tranquility about it, and about her — a quiet, calm spirit — that I have never forgotten, and that I shall never forget.

This was his little housekeeper, his daughter Agnes, Mr Wickfield informed us, and she had assured him she would very much like me to board with them.

"Now David," said my aunt, preparing to leave, "never be mean in anything, never be false, and never be cruel; avoid those three vices and I can always be hopeful of you. Be a credit to yourself, to me and to Mr Dick, and may heaven be with you!"

With these words she embraced me and went out of the room, closing the door after her.

Life at Mr Wickfield's house appeared to be very pleasant and peaceful. After dinner we went upstairs to the drawing-room, in one snug corner of which Agnes set a decanter of port wine and glasses for her father. There he sat, taking a good deal of his wine, for two hours, while Agnes played the piano or talked with us. She appeared to be totally devoted to him, and he to her.

The next morning, after breakfast, Mr Wickfield took me to my new school and introduced me to Dr Strong, the headmaster —a gentleman as different from Mr Creakle as it was possible to be. The head-boy, Adams, showed me round and presented me to the masters in a way that would have put me at ease — if anything could, for I was very conscious of the differences in experience and learning between myself and the other boys.

That evening Agnes told me that her mother had died when she was born, and that now, even at her young age, she considered it her duty to stay at home and keep house for her father.

The evening was much the same as the previous one, and on parting to go to bed Mr Wickfield asked me if I thought I should like to stay on with them. I said I should like to very much, and we shook hands on the arrangement.

On the way out to school the following morning I encountered Uriah Heep sweeping the steps outside the house.

"Good morning, Master Copperfield. I trust you'll have a good day at school."

"Thank you, Uriah, and I hope you'll have a good day with your studies in the law."

"Oh, yes, Master Copperfield. When I have the opportunity I am reading *Tidd's Practice*. What a writer Mr Tidd is, Master Copperfield."

"I suppose you are quite a lawyer?"

"Me, Master Copperfield? Oh no, I'm a very 'umble person. I am well aware that I am the 'umblest person going. Let the other be where he may. Likewise my mother is a very 'umble person. We live in an 'umble abode, Master Copperfield, but have much to be thankful for."

"Have you been with Mr Wickfield long?" I asked, mainly to seem agreeable.

"Going on four year, Master Copperfield, since a year after the death of my father."

"Then, when your articled time is over, you'll be a regular lawyer, I suppose. Perhaps one of these days you'll be a partner in Mr Wickfield's business, and it will be 'Wickfield and Heep'."

"Oh, no, Master Copperfield, I am much too 'umble for that!" His mouth widened and the creases in his cheeks deepened and he wriggled about endlessly, shaking his bony head and twisting his hunched body. "Mr Wickfield is a most excellent man, Master Copperfield. If you have known him long, then you know it better than I can inform you."

I replied that I had not known him long, but that he was a friend of my aunt.

"Oh indeed, Master Copperfield. Your aunt is a sweet lady. She has a great admiration for Miss Agnes, I believe?"

I said 'yes', though I knew nothing about it.

"I hope you have, too, Master Copperfield?"

"Everybody must have, Uriah, I would have thought."

"Oh, thank you, Master Copperfield, for that remark. It is so true! 'Umble as I am, I know it to be true. Oh, thank you!"

I made to walk off but Uriah stopped me. "I suppose you will be staying here some time, Master Copperfield?"

I said I believed I would be there as long as I remained at school.

"Oh, indeed! I should think you would come into the business then, Master Copperfield."

I said that I had no views of the kind, and nor had anybody else, but Uriah kept replying to all my assurances until I was forced to be quite off-hand with him in order to get away.

That day I was a little easier at school, and in two weeks or so I was very contented there. I was awkward enough in their games and backward enough in their studies, but practice would improve me in the first, I hoped, and hard work in the second. Fortunately I was to be proved correct in both these judgments.

Every third or fourth week I visited Aunt Betsey in Dover, and on alternate Wednesdays Mr Dick would visit me. He became great friends with Dr Strong and a popular figure at the school, even though he took no active part in any pursuit except kite-flying. Life at the Wickfield home was suitably quiet — and dear Agnes became more of a sister to me than even Aunt Betsey could ever imagine.

5 I Return to London

I am uncertain whether I was glad or sorry when my schooldays drew to an end and the time came for my leaving Dr Strong's. I had been happy there, and I was distinguished in that tiny world; but misty ideas of being a young man of independence were powerful in me.

My aunt and Mr Dick and I had held many serious deliberations on the calling to which I should be devoted — but I had no particular liking, as far as I could discover, for any sphere of activity.

"It had occurred to me, David," said Aunt Betsey one evening, "that a change may be useful in helping you to know your own mind. Suppose you were to go down to the old part of the country again, and see that woman with the strangest of names."

I was more than happy at this suggestion, and wrote to Peggotty to tell her — the latest in a long line of letters I had sent her.

I bade my farewells and took the coach to London, putting up at the Golden Cross hotel. I was making my way from the coffee-room to go to bed when I passed the person who had just come in, and I knew him in a moment. But he didn't seem to know me.

"Steerforth! Won't you speak to me?"

He turned and looked at me, hesitating in his recognition. "My God! It's little Copperfield!"

We ordered some refreshment and exchanged news. He was on his way from the university at Oxford to his mother's home in Highgate, and when I told him of my plans, he invited me to spend a few days there. I enjoyed a glorious, frivolous week in his inspiring company and, after some hesitation on his part, persuaded him to accompany me to Yarmouth.

Over breakfast at the Dolphin Hotel, we agreed that I would go alone to see Peggotty, and that we would rendezvous at the Barkis' house later in the morning.

"Davy, my darlin' boy!" cried Peggotty on my appearance at her door. "How are you? My, look how you've growed! It's so good to see you. Oh, Barkis will be glad."

After she had dried her eyes she led me inside to see her husband, who was laid up in bed with rheumatism.

enjoyable meal.

On our departure Peggotty was quite insistent that I stay with her during my visit, and my friend concurred. That settled, we made our way through the town and across the sands to the curious boathouse which for two weeks had once been my home. Even as we approached, its three occupants were outside, waving a welcome. "Mas'r Davy!" called out Ham. "It's Mas'r Davy!"

"Hallo, young Davy!" said Mr Peggotty. "It's grand to see you after all this while."

"Hello, Mr Peggotty. Do you remember my friend Steerforth?"

"I do, Davy, I do. He's the sailor and the cricketer."

"Good day, Mr Peggotty, and well met," said Steerforth, shaking him firmly by the hand.

"And this 'ere's Little Em'ly. She ain't my child; I never had one. But I couldn't love her more, you understand?"

"I quite understand," said Steerforth, looking with great interest at Emily. "Well met indeed!"

"But Little Em'ly ain't mine no more. She's engaged to be wed to 'am, these two days past, and will be married when she's of the age!"

After a discussion about her husband's health, Peggotty took me through and began preparing dinner, asking all sorts of questions and apologizing for not having replied to as many of my letters as she would have liked. I, in turn, prepared her for the arrival of Steerforth. Like all others before her, she was charmed by his manner and his humour, and we spent a most

"She weren't no higher than you was, Mas'r Davy, when you come to stay," said Ham, softly. "I see her grown up like a flower. I'd lay down my life for her, gentl'men. She's more to me than — than ever I could say. I love her true. There ain't a man in all the land — nor yet sailing on all the sea — that can love his lady more than I love her, though there's many a common man would say better what he meant."

It was moving to see such a sturdy fellow as Ham trembling in the strength of what he felt for the pretty creature who had won his heart.

"I don't know how long I may live, or how soon I may die," said Mr Peggotty, "but if I was capsized in a gale of wind and it was all up with me, I know I could go down quieter for thinkin' that there's a man ashore that's iron-true to my little Em'ly, and that no wrong can touch my darlin' child while it be as that man lives."

We went inside the boathouse and toasted the couple's happiness with all manner of beverages, and passed a wonderful evening there. Steerforth, while setting up no monopoly of the attention, pioneered all the events, and as always took all before him in his stride.

"A most engaging little beauty!" he said as we left to set off across the sands. "Well, it's a

quaint place and they're quaint company, and it's quite a new sensation to mix with them!"

"How fortunate we are, too," I replied, "to have arrived to witness their happiness. I never saw people so happy!"

"That's a rather chuckle-headed fellow for the girl, isn't he?"

"Ah, Steerforth. It's well for you to joke about the poor. But I know there is not a joy or sorrow they feel that does not affect you."

"David, I believe you are in earnest, and are good. I only wish we all were!"

He suddenly seemed concerned, almost melancholy. "If anything should ever separate us, David, you must think of me at my best. Come, let us make that bargain! Think of me at my best, if circumstances should ever part us!"

"You have no best to me, Steerforth — and no worst. You are always cherished in my heart."

Steerforth and I were together a good deal during our stay, but he often went sailing with Mr Peggotty, while I spent much time with his sister — as well as making two visits to my parents' graves at Blunderstone.

After nearly three weeks we left, and it seemed that half of Yarmouth had come to see us off. The coach journey on the mail was enlivened by two very different topics, the first of which followed an announcement by Steerforth that he had bought a boat in Yarmouth, that Mr Peggotty would be master of her in his absence — and that, in recognition of Mr Peggotty's passion, he had renamed her 'Little Emily'.

The second discussion, and much more lengthy, was the result of a letter that arrived for me at the hotel that morning. It was from Aunt Betsey, staying in London, inviting me to consider entering the law at the Inns of Court.

Steerforth advised me similarly, and when we came to our journey's end I made my way to Holborn, where I found my aunt up and waiting on her supper.

"Well, David," she began, "what do you think of the plan, eh?"

I said I thought it was an excellent plan, but I was concerned that my entrance into that world would prove very expensive.

"It will cost, to article you, two hundred pounds."

I was astonished at the size of the figure, and begged her to consider whether I was worthy of such an investment.

"David, you have been a credit to me — a pride and a pleasure. I have no other claim upon my means, and you are my adopted child. We need talk of this no more. Now give me a kiss, and we'll make our way to the Inns of Court after breakfast tomorrow."

The next morning we walked to the office of Spenlow and Jorkins, where I was introduced to Mr Spenlow and, following a brief interview, taken into employment as an articled clerk, initially on a month's probation. It was all, indeed, a far cry from the cellars of Murdstone and Grinby, though the institutions were less than a mile apart.

From Spenlow and Jorkins my aunt guided me away to Buckingham Street, in the Adelphi, where we were to view a set of chambers advertized as 'a genteel residence for a young gentleman'. These premises were run by a Mrs Crupp, and proved satisfactory. The following day I moved in, and began life on my own account.

6 Love and Hate

I had been in my chambers two weeks or so when I received a short letter from Agnes, entreating me to visit her in Canterbury, so on the following Saturday I took the Dover Mail.

It was a delight to see her, but we had not been together long before she brought up the reason for her request.

"David, I believe that Uriah is going to enter into partnership with Papa."

"What! Uriah? How could that mean, fawning fellow even be considered for such a promotion? You must protest, Agnes, before it's too late!"

"I'm afraid it is too late, David. He has made himself indispensable to Papa. He has mastered Papa's weaknesses, fostered them, and taken advantage of them until Papa is almost frightened of him."

There was more that she could have said on the matter, but I clearly saw she withheld it from me in order to spare her father.

That evening, at supper, Heep hovered around the table, attending to this and that and ensuring that Mr Wickfield's glass was never empty of wine. After the meal, he said he wished to speak with me.

"What a prophet you have shown yourself, Master Copperfield. You have heard something, I dare say, of a change in my expectations,

Master Copperfield."

"Yes, something."

"I have risen from my 'umble station since first you knew me, Master Copperfield, but I am 'umble still. I hope you will not think the worse of my 'umbleness if I make a little confidence to you, Master Copperfield, will you?"

"If you must."

" 'Umble as I am, Master Copperfield, I love Agnes Wickfield!"

I had the delirious idea of seizing the red-hot

poker from the fire and running him through with it. But I contained myself, and asked him, as casually as I could in the circumstances, whether he had made known his feelings to her.

"Oh no, Master Copperfield! Not to anyone but you! You see, I rest a good deal of hope on her observing how useful I am to her father, and how I keep him straight. She's so much attached to her father, Master Copperfield, that I think she may come, on his account, to be kind to me!"

I fathomed the depth of the rascal's whole scheme, and understood why he laid it bare.

The image of Uriah Heep's ugly figure was still fresh in my mind when, the following week, I was articled to the firm of Spenlow and Jorkins. After we had concluded our business, Mr Spenlow said he would be happy to see me at his house in Norwood the weekend after next, when his daughter would have returned from

completing her education in Paris. We were to drive down in his carriage on the Saturday, and return to London on the Monday morning.

As we went into the house that fateful evening, Mr Spenlow asked a servant where Dora was. "Dora!" I thought. "Dora. What a beautiful name!"

We turned into the breakfast room and I heard a voice say, "Mr Copperfield, my daughter Dora." It was, no doubt, Mr Spenlow's voice, but I didn't know and didn't care. All was over in a moment. I had fulfilled my destiny. I was a captive and a slave. I loved Dora Spenlow to distraction!

The remainder of the evening is lost to me. I don't recall who was there, or what was said, or what we had to eat: only her. I sat next to her. I talked to her. She had the most delightful little voice, the loveliest little laugh, the most fascinating little ways, that ever lost a youth into hopeless slavery. I went to bed, and woke up, in a crisis of feeble infatuation.

I was out in the garden, well before breakfast, when I turned a corner and met her. I tingled from head to foot, and my voice shook as I spoke to her. "You are out early, Miss Spenlow."

"On a Sunday morning, when I don't practise the piano, I must do something. Besides, it's the brightest time of the day. Don't you think so, Mister Copperfield?"

I didn't know what to think, and cannot recall what I replied. I only remember than her dog Jip barked and was mortally jealous of me — and that when she picked him up, and patted him, and laid her chin upon his head, I was mortally jealous of him.

The day passed in a haze of adulation, and I was miserable afterwards that I conveyed nothing of my feelings for her. I was always looking out for another invitation, but as each day drifted by and I received none, I became increasingly disappointed.

I was shocked out of this maudlin state of mind by the sudden appearance of a dear friend. He was waiting for me outside the office late one evening as I left for home.

"Hallo, Davy!"

"Mr Peggotty! What a pleasant surprise! What brings you to London?"

"A grave business, Davy. I've come to find my little Em'ly. She's run off with your friend Steerforth! I've come to search for my neice and

that damned villain, and I'll track 'em down, no matter where they hide."

I will not forget that anguished face and the words that it uttered if I live to be five hundred years. The effect this news wrought on me — and the guilt it inspired — I could not describe.

I took Mr Peggotty to my chambers, and there he told me of the dreadful night of her disappearance, of her note to Ham and himself, begging their forgiveness, of the tears and the wailing and the hate that followed.

"We've had a load of talk, Davy, of what we ought and ought not to do. But I see my course clear. I'm goin' to seek my Em'ly far and wide, and return her to her proper home, if it take me to the end of my nat'ral days! That's my dooty evermore. And if any hurt should come to me — remember Davy, remember that the last words I left her was, 'My unchanged love is with my darlin' child, and I forgive 'er!'"

He suddenly seemed fatigued by the emotion of the telling of his story; I asked him if he had found a room to stay, and he said he was fixed up in a place in Pentonville. Offering my assurance that I would be of help in any form I could, I resolved there and then to ask for leave from my employment and travel to Yarmouth — to do whatever was in my power to comfort Peggotty and poor, deserted Ham.

On the journey I could think of little except my own part in this diabolical affair — of how I had introduced Steerforth to these good people and wrecked so many precious lives.

I found Ham before I reached the boathouse, down by the sea, and even from a distance he looked a forlorn, dejected figure. He turned as I approached, and put on a brave face.

"Hallo, Mas'r Davy. It's good to see you."

"Ham, I'm so sorry that —"

"It ain't no fault of yorn, Mas'r Davy. And you han't no call to be afeered of me. It's done, that's all. The pride and hope of my 'art — her that I'd have died for, would die for now — she's gone!"

I looked at him as he gazed out to sea, and a frightful thought came into my mind. Not that his face was angry; it was not. I recall nothing but an expression of stern determination in it: that if he ever encountered Steerforth, he would surely kill him.

It chanced that while I was in Yarmouth another loss befell this sad community. The state of Mr Barkis' health had deteriorated much in the few weeks since my last visit, so that when I went to see Peggotty at her house she cried and told me he was near his end.

She tried gently to rouse him on my account, but he was senseless. We remained in the room, watching him, for some hours.

"He's a-goin' out with the tide," said Ham, suddenly breaking the silence.

I asked him, in a whisper, what he meant.

"People can't die along the coast, except when the tide's pretty nigh out. They can't be born unless it's pretty high in. He's a-goin' out with the tide."

After some minutes he began to move his head and mumble.

"He's coming to himself," said Peggotty, clutching his hand. "Barkis, my dear!"

"Clara Barkis," he murmured. "No better woman anywheres."

"Look! Here's Master Davy, who brought us together, you remember?"

He half opened is eyes, and I was on the point of asking him if he knew me when he tried to stretch out his arm, and said to me, distinctly, with a pleasant smile: "Barkis is willin'."

And, it being low water, he went out with the tide.

I stayed with Peggotty until after Mr Barkis had made his last journey to Blunderstone, where my old nurse had long since bought a little piece of ground in the churchyard. Despite the trying circumstances, I derived a good deal of satisfaction from being a constant source of comfort to Peggotty and from taking charge of Barkis' will. This turned out to be surprisingly substantial for a man of such modest income (nearly three thousand pounds), and his wife, his brother-in-law and Ham were all to receive significant advantage.

The thought of Dora was a great consolation to me in the subsequent weeks in London. The idea of her was my refuge in disappointment and

smiled, and we all seemed, to my thinking, to go straight up to the seventh heaven.

We did not come down again. We stayed up there all the afternoon and evening. For my part I stayed up there for a week, until the occasion of my next call.

As we walked through the gardens, Dora's shy arm through mine, we found ourselves at the greenhouse. Then — I don't know how I did it — but I did it in a moment! I shut out Jip; I had Dora in my arms; I told her how I loved her, how I should die without her. I told her I idolized and worshipped her. And I embraced her and kissed her upon her lips, and she would not let me draw away.

I suppose we had some notion that this would end in marriage. We must have, because Dora stipulated that we were never to be married without her father's consent. We were to keep our secret from Mr Spenlow, but I'm sure the idea never entered my head, then, that there was anything dishonourable in that understanding.

What a happy, foolish time it was that followed! Of all the times of mine, there is none that I can smile at half so much, and think of half so tenderly.

distress, and it seemed that the greater the accumulation of trouble in the world, the brighter her star shone above it. Then, one morning, my prayers were answered.

Following a long and not altogether uninteresting discussion about the law in general with Mr Spenlow, he invited me down a week hence for a picnic to celebrate Dora's birthday. I went out of my senses immediately, and think I committed every possible absurdity in preparation for this blessed event. I blush when I remember the cravat I bought; my boots might have been placed in any collection of instruments of torture; I provided, and sent down by coach the night before, a hamper which amounted almost to a declaration of love.

At six in the morning I was in Covent Garden Market, buying a bouquet, and by ten I was trotting down to Norwood on horseback.

Jip barked at me on my arrival, and when I presented my bouquet he bared his teeth at me. Well he might if he knew how much I adored his exquisite mistress!

"Oh, thank you, Mister Copperfield," said Dora. "What lovely flowers!"

I had been practising to say that I had thought them beautiful — before I saw them so near her. But I just could not manage it. She was too bewildering, and I lost all power of language in a dumb ecstasy.

I regained my ability to speak sufficiently to ask her, during the rather crowded picnic, whether she would do me the honour of taking a walk with me, and she consented. Then I hardly knew what I did, I was burning to that extent. But I took Dora's hand and kissed it, and she

7 Two Dreams Come True

I was still in this blissful state some weeks later when I saw before me in the street a figure who, though unmistakably not from another world, may just as well have been for the advancement in my fortunes since last I had seen him.

"Mr Micawber! Mr Micawber!"

At first he did not know me in the least, though he stood face to face with me. Then he examined my features with more attention, fell back, and cried: "Is it possible? Do I again have the pleasure of beholding Copperfield, the companion of my youth?"

"You do, Mr Micawber. Indeed you do! And how are you — and Mrs Micawber?"

"You find us, Copperfield, established on an unassuming scale. But you are aware that I have, in my career, surmounted difficulties and conquered obstacles. You are no stranger to the fact that there have been periods of my life when it has been requisite that I should fall back, before making what I trust I shall not be accused of presumption in terming — a spring. The present is one of those momentous stages in the life of man. You find me, Copperfield, fallen back, for a spring, and I have every reason to believe that a vigorous leap will shortly be the result."

"I'm sure you will spring like a tiger, Mr

Micawber. In the meantime, could I invite you and your good wife to dine with me in my chambers tomorrow evening at eight o'clock?"

"Young Copperfield in chambers! Oh, Time, you are a thief and a rogue! We should be delighted, my friend, and you may depend upon it that we shall be hungry!"

At the appointed time my guests arrived, and both were delighted with my residence.

"My dear Copperfield, this is luxurious. It is a way of life which reminds me of the period when I was myself in a state of celibacy, and Mrs Micawber had not yet been solicited to plight her faith at the altar."

"He means solicited by him, Mr Copperfield," said Mrs Micawber. "He cannot answer for others."

"Now tell me, Copperfield. With the example of such a tested union as ours before you, have you any thoughts on the twin peaks of human existence — namely love and marriage — to occupy your mind at present?"

"I have indeed, Mr Micawber," I replied, blushing just a little, and I informed them of my love for Dora.

After celebration of this state of affairs with several toasts, the conversation took a more practical turn, with Mrs Micawber extolling the professional abilities, as yet unappreciated, of her dear husband.

We were discussing how these talents could best be brought to the notice of society when there was a knock on the outer door to my rooms. I opened it to be greeted by the astonishing spectacle of my aunt and Mr Dick — she sitting upon a large trunk and he clutching his beloved kite!

"Aunt Betsey! Mr Dick!"

"David!" said my aunt, brusquely. "Have you become firm and self-reliant?"

"I — I hope so, aunt."

"Then why, my dear boy, why do you think I prefer to sit upon this property of mine tonight?"

I shook my head, unable even to guess.

"Because, David, it's all I have. Because I'm ruined, my dear!"

I was still recovering from the shock of this news when there was a voice at my shoulder.

"Fear not, my dear lady!" said Mr Micawber boldly. "I have no scruple in saying that I am a man who has, for some years, contended against the pressures of monetary difficulties. I have been to the land of penury, but I have returned. Madam, all is not lost!"

My aunt seemed not in the least put out by this intrusion, and took it in the spirit in which it had been made. "Your eloquent friend is right, David. We must meet our reverses boldly, and not suffer them to frighten us. We must learn to act the play out. We must live misfortune down!"

At this point Mr Dick clapped his hands several times in appreciation.

I invited my unexpected visitors inside and introduced them to the Micawbers, who, after expressing the appropriate sentiments, left us to our own devices.

My aunt explained that she had become dissatisfied with her financial advisor and had taken it upon herself to make her own investments, through Mr Wickfield's firm. All had ended in failure, she had been informed, and the finish was very sudden. Apart from the belongings still on the landing, all she had in the world was her cottage.

I ventured that I must do something to help her in her distress.

"Go for a soldier, do you mean?" returned my aunt. "Or go to sea? I won't hear of it. We're not going to have any knockings on the head in this family, sir, if you please!"

It was getting late, and we left these grand concerns to talk of more immediate problems. It was decided that I take Mr Dick round to a boarding-house in Hungerford Market, while Aunt Betsey was to stay with me. She was to have my room, and I was to bed down in the sitting-room by the fire, to keep guard over her.

I decided to pay no heed to my aunt's advice — heaven knows she had been generous enough to me — and the next morning I asked Mr Spenlow if I might cancel my articles with his firm and reclaim her investment. He maintained that he himself would have no objection — despite the awkward precedent it would set — but was convinced that his partner, Mr Jorkins, would be quite immovable on such a subject.

That evening I found a letter from Agnes waiting for me in my chambers, the contents of which I found very disturbing. Uriah Heep was now a partner, and he and his dreadful mother had moved into the Wickfield house. I replied by

return to say that I would be down to Canterbury at the very next opportunity.

This mission was delayed by the sudden death of Dora's father, who collapsed in his carriage one evening on the way home to Norwood. The business thus needed extra attention for some weeks — indeed it soon began to fall off quite badly — but my main concern was for my dear sweetheart.

I had now a morbid jealousy of death, that it would keep her from me; and so in a way it did, since she now fell under the protection of two aunts who lived together in Putney. Neither had seen their neice since her christening, but they now assumed responsibility for her welfare and spirited her away.

It was some while until, prompted by the advice of Agnes, I grew sufficiently bold to tell them of our situation; and eventually, after a long and almost paralyzing wait, Dora and myself were officially engaged to be married.

The following week I set off for Canterbury, calling first at Dover to check on the tenants of Aunt Betsey's cottage. Imagine my surprise when, on entering the office now marked 'Wickfield and Heep', I should see none other than Mr Micawber plying his pen at Uriah's old desk! After our customary exchanges, he explained that he had raised the funds necessary to advertize his talents — the great spring to which he had alluded in London — and that one Uriah Heep had engaged him as 'a confidential clerk'.

"And how do you like the law, Mr Micawber?" I asked.

"My dear Copperfield, to a man possessed of the higher imaginative powers, the objection to legal studies is the amount of detail they involve.

Even in our professional correspondence, the mind is not at liberty to soar to any exalted form of expression. Still, it is a great pursuit!"

He then informed me that he had become the tenant of Uriah Heep's former house, and that he and Mrs Micawber were comfortable. But I detected a change in him, as if his duties did not suit him.

On my way to see Agnes I was intercepted by Uriah Heep, who invited — or rather badgered — me into his office. He asked me about my feelings towards Agnes; indeed he was so insistent that I found myself declaring my brotherly love for her, and confessing that I was recently engaged to Dora.

This seemed to please him enormously and at dinner, flushed with new confidence, he enticed Mr Wickfield into a series of toasts. Finally, when Agnes had left us, he raised his glass and in a gesture of triumph said, "Gentlemen, I give you Agnes Wickfield, the divinest of her sex! To be her father is a proud distinction, but to be her 'usband —"

"No! No!" cried Mr Wickfield, his face distorted with impotent rage. "Look at my torturer! Before him I have, step by step, abandoned name and reputation, house and home! Oh, see the millstone he is about my neck!"

"You had better stop him, Copperfield, if you can," sneered Uriah, pointing. "He'll say something presently he'll be sorry to have said afterwards, and you'll be sorry to 'ave 'eard!"

I did not even have to consider stopping him, because at that moment the door opened and Agnes came in. She helped her distraught father out of his chair and up to the drawing-room.

The next morning, over breakfast, I pleaded with Agnes not to marry Heep from a mistaken sense of duty; but despite my protestations, she would not give me that promise.

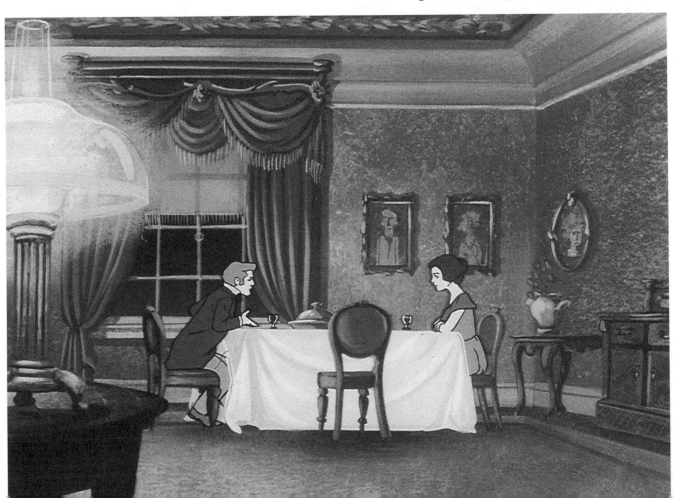

Shortly after this unhappy episode, Dora and I were married. Few attended the wedding and when the guests had left we settled down to married life. I must confess that Dora found domestic chores uncongenial; indeed, despite the advice and help first of Peggotty and then Aunt Betsey, she never ever began to master the art of managing the household.

Life too changed for me. What had once been just a hobby — writing stories for magazines — soon became a full-time occupation and by the end of the year I left the employment of Spenlow and Jorkins to devote myself to my first novel.

It was on the penultimate day of my stay at Spenlow and Jorkins that I unexpectedly met Mr Peggotty. It was a cold night, so I invited him to a tavern so that we could talk.

This tireless wanderer had been away for some months, searching alone for his beloved Emily and her lover. He had been to France, to Italy, to Switzerland, nearly always travelling on foot, and had come close to finding them on more than one occasion. But the trail had disappeared, and now he had come back to London, via Yarmouth.

Whilst in London he had discovered from a girl named Martha, who was also from Yarmouth, the whereabouts of his young neice.

"Martha's to meet me on the north side of Westminster Bridge tomorrow night, at ten," said Mr Peggotty, "and take me to my darlin' child. I'd be more than happy if you'd come with me, Davy, if you can!"

We met Martha at the appointed time. In complete silence she led us along the murky waterfront. After some time, she darted into a dark entrance and up some stairs to the second floor of an old house. Still not a word was spoken. We opened the door and stood inside, waiting. A thin, frightened figure appeared from behind a screen, and peered at us for a moment. "Uncle!"

A fearful cry followed the word; then, with a start, Emily fell insensible, into the arms of Mr Peggotty. He gazed for a few seconds into her face, then kissed her gently.

"Davy," he said quietly, looking up at me. "I thank my 'eavenly father as my dream's come true! I thank him hearty for guidin' me, in his own strange ways, to my darlin' child!"

With those words he took her up in his arms and carried her, motionless and still unconscious, down the broken stairs and out into the dark night.

The next day Mr Peggotty came round to see

me. "All night long," he began, the tears welling in his eyes, "her arms have been about my neck, and we knows full well that we can trust each other ever more. I want to thankee, Davy, for coming last night, and for being my friend."

He told me that at first Emily and Steerforth had indeed ventured all over Europe; but in Naples — he growing restless and she becoming melancholy — he had abandoned her. She had worked her own passage home, finally encountering her old friend Martha on the streets of London.

"And what of the future, Mr Peggotty?"

"I've made up my mind, Davy, and told little Em'ly. There's mighty countries, far from here, and our future lies over the sea. No-one can't reproach my darlin' in Australia. We sail in six weeks. But there's one thing more, Davy. I can't take Em'ly to Yarmouth and I can't leave her here, neither; so I've writ letters to Clara and Ham, setting everything down. Could you take them for me, Davy, and take my farewell leave of Yarmouth for me?"

As on my previous visit, it was easy to come Ham's way, and I told him all that had happened in London.

"When you see her, Mas'r Davy," said Ham, "there's somethin' I could wish said. It ain't that I forgive her — it ain't that so much. 'Tis more that I beg *her* to forgive *me*, for havin' pressed my

affections on her. Odd times I think that if I hadn't had her promise to marry me, she might have told me what was struggling in her mind, and I might have saved her."

"Is there anything more?" I asked.

"Yes, Mas'r Davy. The last you see of him — the very last — will you give him the lovingest duty and thanks of the orphan, as he was ever more than a father to?"

I promised faithfully to convey both these messages, and set off to see Peggotty.

8 Gains and Losses

Soon after my return from Yarmouth there arrived a letter from Mr Micawber, in which he implored Aunt Betsey, Mr Dick and myself to be at his office at half-past nine the next day but one, about a matter of the utmost importance. He claimed that our presence was essential to his design, and that it was to our advantage to attend.

I was somewhat uneasy about leaving Dora to obey this strange call, since she was in some distress with a mild fever, but she insisted that both my aunt and myself travel to Canterbury.

We were greeted at the door of Wickfield and Heep by Mr Micawber, who now seemed more like his old self once more.

"Mr Micawber," said Aunt Betsey, "perhaps you would be so good as to tell us why you have called us here today?"

"To expose villainy and corruption, my dear lady," replied Mr Micawber, pointing to the skies, "and to restore your fortunes. Two noble causes, I think you will agree! Now, please step this way."

He led us in and, without knocking, opened the door to Uriah's office. The occupant rose from his chair as Mr Micawber ushered us in. Our visit astonished him, evidently — not the least, I dare say, because it astonished ourselves — but in a moment he had recovered and was as fawning as ever.

"Well, well, this is indeed an unexpected pleasure, I'm sure. Things have changed since I was an 'umble clerk in this office, Miss Trotwood, 'aven't they? But I 'aven't changed, Miss Trotwood."

"No," returned my aunt, coldly. "I think you have been pretty constant to the promise of your youth, if that's any satisfaction to you."

"Oh thank you, Miss Trotwood," replied Uriah, writhing in his ungainly manner and turning to his clerk. "Don't wait, Micawber."

Mr Micawber, with his hand upon a ruler in his breast pocket, stood erect before the door.

"What are you waiting for, Micawber? Go along, I'll talk to you presently."

"If there is a scoundrel on this earth with whom I have already talked too much," said Mr Micawber, leaning slightly forward, "that scoundrel's name is — *Heep!*"

Uriah fell back, as if he had been struck or stung. "Oho, this is a conspiracy! You have met here by appointment. You are playing games with my clerk, Copperfield, are you? Well take care, for I'll counterplot you!"

"Mr Micawber," I said grandly, "you may deal with this fellow as he deserves."

Mr Micawber produced from his pocket a document folded in the form of a letter, and began to read: "In an accumulation of want, despair, shame and madness, I entered the office of the firm called Wickfield and Heep, but in reality wielded by Heep alone. Heep, and only Heep, is the mainspring of that machine, and Heep, and only Heep, is the forger and the cheat!"

"The devil take you, Micawber!" cried Uriah, taking a grab at the letter and receiving a crack with the ruler on his knuckles. "I'll be even with you!"

"Approach me again, you — you — Heep of infamy, and if your head is human, I'll break it. Come on, come on!"

I think I never saw anything more ridiculous — I was aware of it, even at the time — than Mr Micawber's gestures against his cringing enemy. When I had cooled him down, he continued with his letter.

"Soon after entering the employment of Wickfield and Heep I found the salary of twenty-two shillings and sixpence insufficient to alleviate the poverty of my family. I than sank into a state of indebtedness to the snake Heep in the form of IOUs. In return for securing these I was called upon to forge the signature of Mr Wickfield in the pursuit of defrauding both himself and his clients, including Miss Trotwood."

Mr Micawber then read out a long list of specific charges against Heep and put down the letter. "All this I undertake to show," he concluded with a flourish, "and I have the necessary documentation in my possession!"

Suddenly Uriah took out a large key and opened the safe. It was empty.

"All the books are in good hands!" said Mr Micawber.

"So, Heep," said my aunt after a pause, "it is

you who have ruined me!"

"Fear not, dear lady!" cried Mr Micawber. "All shall be returned to you!"

I suggested that Heep be confined to his room until matters were completed, but he agreed only after my aunt threatened to fetch two officers of the law. She then turned her attention to the delicate question of Mr Micawber's future.

"Mr Micawber, I wonder if you have ever turned your thoughts to emigration? It seems to me that Australia would be a legitimate sphere of action for your talents. And I'm sure my present good fortune could suffer a substantial loan."

"Madam, I hear the call of the wild, and the call is Australia!"

We returned home in understandably high spirits. But the euphoria was short-lived, for Dora was now desperately ill, and in a matter of days it became obvious to all that she would not recover. I hardly left her side, but there was nothing I could do. Impotently, I watched her slip away from me. Weak as she was, she begged me to send for Agnes. The two saw each other alone and what was said was not revealed to me until much later. But when Agnes came back downstairs, it was, I knew, all over — I had lost my darling for ever.

Gradually, as I began to recover from the depths of my misery, it was proposed that I go abroad. But it was to Yarmouth that I turned.

The day after Dora's funeral, and in response to the message I conveyed from Ham to Emily, Mr Peggotty showed me a note from Emily to Ham. She had requested that I read it — it was the most touching of communications — and take

charge of it, in case of reply. Under the circumstances I was even more glad than usual to be of service and set off on the coach down the road I had travelled in so many different moods and in so many varied causes.

Yet never had I seen a sky like this one — on this road or indeed anywhere. There had been a strong wind all day, but as afternoon passed into evening it rose higher and higher, and sweeping gusts of rain came up like showers of steel.

I put up at the Dolphin Hotel, then went in search of Ham along the windswept shore; but he was not at his house, nor the yard where he worked. I began to feel an uneasiness about his not being there when I saw a great commotion down by the shore — and then, through the waves and the foam, the sight of a ship pitching and rolling in the heaving seas.

In all the shouting and the noise I made out that she was a schooner from Spain or Portugal, loaded with fruit and wine, and that some crew were still thought to be on board. The lifeboat had been manned an hour since but could make no contact, and as no man had attempted to make off from the boat with a rope and try to establish communication with the shore, there was nothing more to be done.

Then the crowd parted and Ham strode forward, a rope over his shoulder. I ran to him, imploring him not to go, then pleading with his fellow men not to let him. But I might as well have entreated the wind.

"If my time is come, Mas'r Davy, 'tis come," he said, grasping me with both hands. "If it ain't, I'll bide it. Lord above bless you, and bless all! Mates, make me ready. I'm a-going off!"

Ham watched the sea until there was a great retiring wave; then, with a backward glance at those who held the rope made fast round his body, he dashed in after it, and in a moment was buffeting with the water; rising with the hills, falling with the valleys, lost beneath the foam; then drawn again to land. They hauled it hastily.

He was hurt. I saw blood on his face, but he took no thought of it. He seemed to give them directions for leaving him more free, and was then gone as before.

Now he made for the wreck, striving hard and valiantly. The distance was nothing, but the power of the sea and wind made the strife deadly. At length he reached the wreck. He had, somehow, managed to pull himself aboard,

when a vast hillside of water moving on shoreward from beyond the ship engulfed it, and it was gone.

They drew him to my very feet — insensible — dead. Every means of restoration were tried, but all in vain. He had been beaten to death by the great wave, and his generous heart was stilled for ever.

I knelt down beside him, the note from Emily gripped in my hand. I looked up to see another body being carried up the beach. They laid the poor wretch down next to Ham, his head resting on his arm.

I thought at first sight that my mind was confused by tragedy and long exposure to the fierce wind and great roar of the storm; but I was not mistaken. On that part of the beach where I had looked for shells with Emily, on that part of it where some lighter fragments of the old boathouse, blown down by the storm, had been scattered by the wind, among the ruins of the home he had wronged — I saw Steerforth lie with his head upon his arm, as I had so often seen him lie at school.

The effect these two grievous losses had on me — and so soon after the angel of death had taken Dora — I cannot begin to describe. I resolved to adopt my initial idea and go abroad to write, and following the safe departure of the emigrants from Gravesend — the Micawber family, Mr Peggotty, Emily and Martha — I travelled slowly to Switzerland, leaving behind all those who

were dear to me.

The solitude seemed to increase the power of my pen, and in a short time I became not only a successful novelist but also quite a famous one.

The great joy in my lonely life were the letters of Agnes, and as the time passed and my third summer abroad approached, I began to realize that my love for her — a very different love from

that I had felt for Dora — was far more than that of a brother, and always had been.

And so I returned to Dover, and the very next day rode to Canterbury. I had nurtured fears about Agnes being committed to another, about her not seeing me in the same light as I now saw her. But all these were ill-founded. She was as gentle and charming as ever; and when I confessed that I felt for her more than a mere brother, she said that she had to confess to me that she had always felt more than a sister should to me. We spoke no more words, but sealed our new love with a kiss.

How happy we were! How right it all seemed! We were soon married, and as we rode away, through the gates of Canterbury, Agnes turned to me and said: "Dearest husband! Now that I may call you that, I have one thing more to tell you. On the night Dora died, she made a last request to me, and left me a last charge."

"And what was it, my darling?"

"That only I would occupy this vacant place."

And Agnes laid her head upon my breast, and wept; and I wept with her, though we were so very happy.

Epilogue

There is yet one incident which I must relate to complete my record.

I had advanced in fame and fortune and been married ten wonderful years. Agnes and I were sitting by the fire in our London home, and three of our children were playing in the room, when I was told that a stranger wished to see me.

It was no stranger: it was none other than Mr Peggotty. An old man now, but in a ruddy, hearty, strong old age. When our first emotion was over, and he sat before the fire with the children on his knees, he told us of our friends' fortunes in Australia.

They had all fared well, by all accounts, in the change from the sea to the land. Emily was with him, at home, always the first to do someone a kindness, and constantly turning down offers of marriage; Martha, however, had married in their second year, to a farm labourer who lived four hundred miles off in the bush land.

Mr Micawber and his family had worked as hard as Mr Peggotty had seen anyone work, and he had at last achieved the position of respect he desired. The visitor produced a copy of the local paper as illustration, and indeed Mr Micawber's influence was everywhere in it, not least in the report of a public dinner 'in honour of our distinguished townsman and magistrate'. There was also a letter in the paper from the said gentleman and addressed to *David Copperfield, Esq., the eminent author*, in which he sent the greetings of himself and his community.

Before Mr Peggotty left for Australia a month later he went with me to Yarmouth, to see a tablet I had put up in the churchyard to the memory of Ham. While I was copying the plain inscription for him, at his request, I saw him stoop and gather a tuft of grass from the grave.

"For Em'ly," he said, as he put it in his breast. "I promised, Davy."

We also journeyed to Dover, to see his sister — wearing spectacles now and a good deal thinner, but still my old nurse, and still a housekeeper. And Aunt Betsey, an old woman of four-score years and more but upright yet, and a steady walker of six miles at a stretch in winter weather. Her old disappointment is set right now, for she is godmother to a real living Betsey Trotwood; and Dora (the next in order) says she spoils her. And Mr Dick, making giant kites among my sons, and taking me aside to whisper in my ear that "your aunt's the most extraordinary woman in the world, sir!"

And what of those far from dear to me? Uriah Heep made off with his mother to London, not without funds, but is at present residing in a Middlesex prison after convictions for fraud, forgery and conspiracy. Power, not money, was always his ambition.

Of the Murdstones I know only because the doctor who delivered this writer into the world has moved to the village where they now reside near Bury St Edmunds. He married yet another lively young woman and now he and his sister have also destroyed her with their gloom and austerity. They go about with her, it is said, more like her keepers than her husband and sister-in-law. I can all too easily believe it to be the sorry truth.

But one face, shining on me like a heavenly light by which I shall see all other objects, is above all. I turn my head and see it, in its beautiful serenity, beside me. O, Agnes, so may thy face be by me when I close my life.

Great Expectations

Introduction

SEVERAL of Dickens' novels are about "great expectations" since they have as their central theme the rags-to-riches story of a poor, underprivileged boy who is finally accepted into polite society. It is strange then, given the happy endings of both *Oliver Twist* and *David Copperfield*, that *Great Expectations* ends with the main character, Pip, being stripped of his wealth and his position in society.

Unlike *Oliver Twist* and *David Copperfield*, whom we come to like and even admire, Pip is not really a hero. Despite his virtues, he becomes a snob and is corrupted by his good fortune. Suddenly removed from his labours in a country smithy and sent to London to be educated as a gentleman, he is impressed by the wrong people for the wrong reasons. He neglects and abandons the honest, hardworking folk who have always cared for him, he is irritated and embarrassed by the gentle blacksmith Joe Gargery, and his pride is hurt when he learns who his mysterious benefactor is.

But Pip's snobbery is not blind or callous; he is aware of it and often expresses guilt for his behaviour. In the end his feelings for the convict Magwitch are our own: fear of his violent nature and a dislike of his crude ways, but admiration for his courage.

For many years Pip is kept in ignorance of his benefactor. Is it the frightening Miss Havisham, deserted on her wedding day and living in a mansion of memories and cobwebs? Is it the sinister Mr Jaggers, the lawyer who pays Pip his generous allowance? And for years Pip nurses a fascination for the icy and beautiful Estella, trained by Miss Havisham to "break men's hearts". Perhaps because his good fortune has come to him so easily, Pip is not a man who makes many friends, apart that is from the cheerful Herbert Pocket.

Written in 1860 and 1861, in the twilight of his life, *Great Expectations* was the thirteenth of Dickens' fourteen major novels, and it marked a return to more familiar territory after his excursions abroad in *A Tale of Two Cities*. From the very start — it has the most dramatic and gripping start of all Dickens' novels — it unfolds a story that drives eagerly forward, full of emotion and humour, and full — as always in Dickens — of unforgettable characters.

1 Strange Encounters

My father's surname being Pirrip, and my Christian name being Philip, I could make little of either when I was very young except 'Pip'. So I called myself Pip, and came to be called Pip.

I give Pirrip as my family name on the authority of my father's tombstone and that of my sister, Mrs Joe Gargery, who married the blacksmith. As I never saw my father or mother, nor a picture of them, my first impressions were inspired by their tombstone. The shape of the letters gave me the idea that my father was a square, stout man; and from the inscription *'Also Georgina, Wife of the Above'*, I drew the conclusion that my mother was freckled and sickly. Next to their grave were five stone tablets, each about a foot and a half long, sacred to the memory of five brothers of mine, all of whom gave up the struggle for life before they had reached an age to talk.

The bleak churchyard holding the graves was set on a low hill in the wilderness of the marsh country where I lived — flat country intersected with dykes and mounds and ditches. Beyond it was the winding river, and beyond that, some twenty miles away, was the sea.

As I knelt before my parents' grave on that raw afternoon, towards evening on Christmas Eve, I suddenly felt more alone and more helpless than I had ever felt before in my life, and I began to cry.

"Hold your noise!" cried a terrible voice. "Keep still, you little devil, or I'll cut your throat!"

Next to me there was now a fearful man, all in coarse brown, with irons round his legs; a man who limped and shivered, and glared and growled, and whose teeth chattered in his head as he seized me with his great hands.

"Don't cut my throat, sir!" I pleaded in terror, my face only inches from his. "Please don't, sir!"

"Tell us your name, boy! Quick!"

"Pip, sir!"

"Show us where you live. Point out the place!"

"Over there, sir," I said, pointing to our village. "About a mile away."

"Where's your mother?"

"There, sir. She's in her grave. And my father."

"Who do you live with, then — supposing you're let to live, which I ain't made up my mind about?"

"My sister, sir — Mrs Joe Gargery — wife of the blacksmith."

"Blacksmith, eh?"

The man looked down at the irons on his legs,

then back at me, and then took me by both arms and tilted me back on a tombstone.

"Now look'ee here. You know what a file is?"

"Yes, sir."

"Well you get me a file, and you get me some victuals. And you bring 'em to me here, early tomorrow morning. You do it, and you never dare say a word to no-one, or I'll have your heart and liver. Now, be off!"

He let go of me suddenly. Then I ran out of the graveyard, down the hill to the road and all the way home without stopping.

Home was a wooden house, with Joe's stone forge joined to it. He was a simple, good-natured, sweet-tempered, easy-going fellow, and I always treated him as a larger kind of child, and as no more than my equal.

My sister was more than twenty years older than I, and had established a great reputation with herself and the neighbours because she had brought me up 'by hand'. Having at that time yet to find out what the expression meant, and knowing her to have a hard and heavy hand, and

to be as much in the habit of laying it on her husband as on me, I supposed that Joe Gargery and I were both brought up 'by hand'.

She was not a good-looking woman, my sister. She was tall and scraggy, and I had the general impression that she must have made Joe marry her 'by hand'.

When I entered the house that cold afternoon, my heart racing with the thought of the task before me, Joe was at the table and my sister was cooking supper. She turned and waved her great ladle at me.

"There you are, you beast of a boy! You'll wear me out with fret and worry, you will. Where have you been?"

"I've — I've been to the churchyard."

"To the churchyard!" repeated my sister, grabbing me by the ear and dumping me on my stool. "If it weren't for me you'd have been to the churchyard long ago, and stayed there under a stone. Who brought you up by hand?"

"You did."

"And why did I do it, I should like to know? I'd never do it again, I know that. I may truly say

I've not had this apron off since you were born. It's bad enough to be a blacksmith's wife, without being your mother!"

Though I was hungry, I dared not eat my hunk of bread and butter, since I knew Mrs Joe was a strict housekeeper and I may find little food available later. So I took advantage of Joe's going to poke the fire to slip the bread under my shirt.

When he sat down again, Joe looked at me in wonder.

"You'll do yourself a mischief, Pip, old chap. It'll stick somewhere. You can't have chewed it!"

"Been bolting his food, has he?" cried my sister, pulling me up by the hair. "You come along and be dosed."

Mrs Joe always kept a supply of tar-water in the cupboard, and at the best of times so much of the mixture was administered to me that I was conscious of going round smelling like a new fence. But the urgency of this occasion demanded a pint of the mixture, poured down my throat while Mrs Joe held my head under her arm. Joe was made to swallow half a pint because 'he had had a turn'; I should say he certainly had a turn afterwards, if he had not had one before.

I was warming myself by the fire before going to bed, when there was the sound of a great gun being fired.

"There's another convict off!" said Joe.

"What does that mean?" I asked.

"Escaped!" said my sister. "Escaped!"

"There was a convict off last night after sunset-gun," explained Joe. "And they fired warning of him. And now it seems they're firing warning of another."

"Who's firing."

"Drat the boy!" interposed my sister. "Ask no questions and you'll be told no lies."

My curiosity, spurred by the meeting at the churchyard, made me far braver than usual.

"Mrs Joe, I should very much like to know where the firing comes from."

"Lord bless the boy!" exclaimed my sister, meaning the very opposite. "From the hulks!"

"Please — what's the hulks?"

"That's the way with this boy! Answer him a question and he'll ask you a dozen more. Hulks are prison-ships, moored across the marshes."

"I wonder who's put into prison-ships, and why they're put there," I said.

My last query seemed too much for Mrs Joe, and she hovered over me, glaring. "People are put into hulks because they murder, and rob, and forge, and do all sorts of bad; and they always begin by asking questions. Now, get along to bed!"

I slept little, fearing now that the hulks were also for me: I had begun by asking questions, after all, and I was going to rob Mrs Joe! But the threat of the man with the irons on his leg seemed even greater, and as soon as daylight appeared at my window the next morning, I sneaked downstairs.

The pantry was far better supplied than usual, owing to Christmas, and I took a piece of cheese,

half a jar of mincemeat, some brandy from a stone bottle and a handsome pork pie.

There was a door from the kitchen into Joe's forge. I unbolted it, and found a file among his tools. I put it under my belt and made off across the misty marshes.

117

It was not yet full light when I reached the churchyard, but I could make out a figure sitting on the first tombstone, his back towards me, and nodding forward as if asleep. I went up and touched him on the shoulder. He jumped up and spun round! It was not the same man, but another!

Yet this man was dressed in coarse brown, too, and was everything the other was, except that he was thinner and had a scar on his face. He swore an oath at me, made a lunge at me, missed — and stumbled out of the churchyard and away down the hill to the marshes.

I had gone only a few more paces when the other man appeared — hugging himself and limping, his body shaking with cold and his face pale with hunger.

"What's in the bottle, boy?"

"Brandy."

He was already eating the bread, and stopped to take some of the liquor. He shivered violently all the while, and it was as much as he could do to keep the bottle between his teeth.

He was soon eating everything at once, like a hungry dog, but breaking off now and again to stop and look around him and listen to the wind.

"Brought anyone with you, boy?"

"No, sir! I swear it!"

He carried on devouring the food, wasting some in his haste, when I timidly asked him if he was going to leave any for the other one.

"Other one? What other one?"

"The other convict. He was here, just now."

"What did he look like?" he said, standing up.

"His face was hurt, sir, on his cheek."

"Where is he? Show me the way he went! I'll pull him down like a bloodhound!"

He tried to move in the direction I was pointing, but the irons brought him down.

"Curse these irons! Give me the file, boy. Quick!"

I handed him the file and in a moment he was working at the chain between the cuffs.

"I'll hunt him down. I'll hunt that gentleman down and feed him to the dogs. I'll get him before they get me! Compeyson! I'm coming after you — you hear me? I'll get you!"

I told him I must go, but he took no notice, so I slipped away. The last I saw of him, his head was bent over his knees and he was working in a frenzy at his fetter; the last I heard of him, when I stopped at the bottom of the hill, he was still shouting curses at the chain and his bleeding legs, and the file was still going.

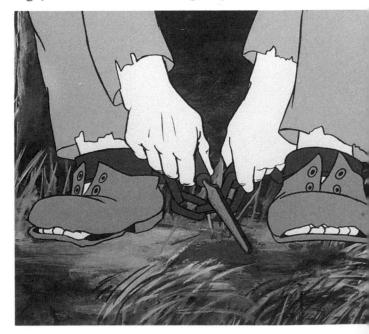

I fully expected to find a constable in the kitchen when I returned. But not only was there no officer; no discovery had yet been made of the theft. Mrs Joe was busy getting the house ready for the day, and when I walked in she was vigorously sweeping the floor.

"And where the deuce have you been?" was her seasonal greeting to me.

"Merry Christmas, Mrs Joe," I replied. "I've been down to the village to hear the carols."

"Carols, is it? Well, you might have done worse. Perhaps if I weren't a slave with her apron never off, I should have been to hear them. I'm rather partial to carols myself."

My sister having so much to do, Joe and I were then ordered to clean up, get changed and go off to church, before coming back for our Christmas dinner.

We were to have a superb meal of leg of pickled pork and greens and a roast stuffed fowl, followed by mince pie and pudding. The table was to be blessed, as usual, with the presence of Uncle Pumblechook. He was Joe's uncle, a well-to-do corn chandler in the nearest town who drove his own smart chaise-cart, and he always brought wine and money on Christmas Day. He was a plump, hard-breathing man, with a mouth like a fish, and an appetite to match his girth. After the pudding Mrs Joe asked him if he had had enough to eat.

"After such a feast, madam, I doubt if I shall break bread until the New Year!"

"Oh, that's a shame then, Uncle Pumblechook. I laid aside a pork pie, especially for you."

"Well! In that case it would be impolite of me to refuse. Just a small piece, mind."

I held tight to the table leg, awaiting the discovery, as my sister went to the pantry. After an age she came back, her face reddening. "The pie — it's gone! The pie's *gone!*"

"Gone?" repeated Uncle Pumblechook. "Gone?"

My sister glared at me, her hands on her hips, and I knew the game was up. I stood, prepared for the worst, when there was a noise outside the house and a loud knock on the door. I was only too happy to take advantage, and ran to open it. It was a sergeant of the army, and in his hand he held a pair of handcuffs.

119

"Excuse me for interrupting on such a day," he said, putting a hand on my shoulder, "but I am on a chase in the name of the King, and I need the blacksmith."

"I'm the blacksmith," said Joe proudly. "What's the trouble, sergeant?"

"We've had an accident with these cuffs, and the coupling ain't working. Could you cast your eyes over 'em — they're wanted for immediate service."

Joe looked at them and said the repair would take an hour or so; then, aided by me, he set to work. In just under an hour — during which time both hosts and visitors drank several glasses of the wine brought by Uncle Pumblechook — the roaring and the ringing in the forge stopped, and the soldiers prepared to leave.

The sergeant suggested to Joe that he might like to go along, and take me with him. Joe asked my sister and, to my great surprise, she agreed, but with one parting shot: "If you bring the boy back with his head blown to bits by a musket, don't look to me to put it together again!"

So off we set, and when we were out in the cold air and moving on, I whispered to Joe: "I hope we shan't find them, Joe!" And he whispered to me: "Pip, old chap, I'd give a shilling if they have cut and run!"

We went first to the churchyard, which was searched, and then struck out across the marshes. Now we were in the wilderness I considered for the first time whether, if we should come upon them, my convict would

suppose it was I who had brought the soldiers to him.

Suddenly we all heard noises, shouting a fair way off — at least two voices. Then we heard a soldier yell, "There they are, the both of 'em!"; and we ran behind the sergeant to the top of the mound. Below him, in the mire, the two convicts were fighting like wild beasts. The sergeant pointed his gun in the air and fired.

"Surrender, you two! Come asunder!"

The two prisoners struggled to their feet, panting and bleeding.

"Mind this!" said my convict. "I took him. I give him up to you!"

"It'll do you little good," said the sergeant, "being in the same plight. Handcuffs there!"

"I don't expect it to do me any good. I took him and he knows it. That's good enough for me."

"He tried to — to murder me!" gasped the other one. "You bear witness!"

"Look'ee here!" said my convict to the sergeant. "Single-handed I got clear of the ship. And I would have got clear of these death-cold flats if I hadn't made the discovery that he was here. Let him go free? Oh no! I held him in that grip that you could find him safe."

"Enough of this!" snapped the sergeant. "It's getting dark. Light them torches!"

As the torches were being prepared, my convict turned and saw me. He gave me a look I did not understand, but it all passed in a moment, and he never looked at me again.

121

"All right!" shouted the sergeant. "March!"

"Hold up," said my convict. "There's something I want to say. It may stop some persons being suspected because of me."

"You can say what you like," replied the sergeant, "but you've no call to say it here, in this forsaken place. You'll have opportunity enough before it's all done with, you know that."

"But this is a separate matter. A man can't starve — at least I can't. I took some victuals, up at the village over yonder, near where the church stands out of the marshes."

"You mean *stole*," said the sergeant.

"Yeah, stole. From the blacksmith's."

"Hallo!" said the sergeant, staring at Joe.

"Hallo," said Joe, staring at me.

"It was some broken victuals, and a dram of liquor, and a pie. That's what it was."

"Have you happened to miss such an article as a pie, blacksmith?" asked the sergeant.

"My wife did, didn't she, Pip?"

"So you're the blacksmith, are you?" said the convict, turning his eyes on Joe, but without the least glance at me. "Then I'm sorry that I ate your pie."

"God knows you're welcome to it," returned Joe, "so far as it was ever mine. We don't know what you've done wrong, but we wouldn't have you starved to death for it, a poor fellow creature. Would us, Pip?"

As I shook my head in silent agreement the procession began its journey back to the prison-ship, with Joe and I at the rear. Soon I could walk no more, and the last thing I remember of that strange, sad day was climbing on to Joe's broad back as we parted ways from the soldiers and their miserable captives.

2 Satis House

I do not recall feeling guilty towards Mrs Joe when the fear of being found out was lifted off me. But I loved Joe — perhaps for no better reason than because the dear fellow let me love him — and I thought that I should tell him the whole truth, particularly when I first saw him looking about for his lost file. Yet I did not, for the fear of losing Joe's confidence, of losing my companion and friend, tied up my tongue.

Life all too quickly returned to normal after Christmas and the excitement of the convicts. When I was old enough I was to be apprenticed to Joe, and in the meantime my schooling consisted of an hour each evening in the room above the general shop of the village.

Our teacher was the great aunt of Mr Wopsle, a friend of my sister's and a clerk of the church,

and she had an orphaned grand-daughter called Biddy. Though only the same age as me, Biddy all but ran the shop for her grandmother as far as I could make out, and she was very clever. It was partly because of Biddy's help, as well as my own efforts, that I struggled through the alphabet as if it had been a bramble-bush, getting scratched by every letter, and learned my tables.

I could expect no help from Joe, since his blacksmith father — a drunkard who used to beat both Joe and his mother horribly — had never allowed him to learn. Joe told me all about his wretched childhood one evening around this time, when he had been impressed by my progress at writing, and I loved him all the more after hearing it.

The day after this talk, I was told by my sister that Uncle Pumblechook wished to speak to me in the sitting-room on a matter of importance.

"You have heard of Miss Havisham, Pip?" he asked, as he stood by the window.

"Yes, sir." Everybody had heard of Miss Havisham as an immensely rich and grim lady who lived a life of seclusion in a large house.

"Miss Havisham is a lady of considerable wealth, and she has sought my advice. 'Mr Pumblechook,' says she, 'do you know of any boy who would be able to come here and play?' 'I do, ma'am,' I replied, 'and his name is Pip.'"

"So that's where you're going," said my sister. "You're to go to town with Uncle Pumblechook

ablutions were completed, I was handed over to Mr Pumblechook, who formally received me as if he were the sheriff. "Be forever grateful to all friends, boy," he said gravely, "but especially unto them that brought you up by hand!"

Joe, who appeared to be as confused by all the activity as I was, came out to see me off. "You'd best do as they say, Pip. God bless you, old chap."

"Goodbye, Joe!"

I had never been parted from him before, and I was confused, wondering why on earth I was going to play at Miss Havisham's, and what on earth I was expected to play at.

We set out in the cart the next morning at ten o'clock, the short journey being taken up — as the dreary breakfast had been — with a series of sums asked by Mr Pumblechook.

Miss Havisham's house was vast and dismal, with many iron bars in it, and some of the windows bricked up. The gate to the courtyard was locked, so we had to wait until someone came to open it. As we waited I noticed that the clock on the tower of the old disused brewery was stopped on twenty minutes to nine o'clock.

"What name?" said a young voice from the

this evening, and he'll take you with his own hands to Miss Havisham's house in the morning. Your fortune could be made by this, so you mind your manners!"

With that she pounced on me, like an eagle on a lamb, and my face was squeezed into sinks, and my head was put under taps, and I was soaped, and kneaded, and rasped and towelled until I was almost beside myself. When these

other side of the gate.

"Pumblechook."

"Quite right," said the voice, and the gate was opened. The owner of the voice was a young lady, who was very pretty and seemed very proud.

"This," said Mr Pumblechook, "is Pip."

"This is Pip, is it? Well come in, Pip."

Mr Pumblechook made to come in too, but the girl stopped him with the gate. "Oh! Do you wish to see Miss Havisham?"

"If Miss Havisham wishes to see me," replied Mr Pumblechook.

"Ah, but you see — she don't!"

This was said so finally that Mr Pumblechook raised no protest. But he was severely ruffled, and departed with the words: "Boy! Let your behaviour here be a credit upon them that brought you up by hand!"

My young guide locked the gate and led me across the courtyard. I stopped to look at the old brewery that was at the side of the house, now empty and decaying, and then up at the inscription on the main door: 'Satis House'.

"Where does the name come from, miss?"

"It's Greek, or Latin, or Hebrew, or all three for 'enough'."

"Enough House! That's a curious name, miss."

"It meant, when it was given, that whoever had this house could want for nothing else. They must have been easily satisfied in those days, I should think. But come on now, boy. Don't loiter!"

Though she called me 'boy' she was only a little older than myself. She seemed a good deal older, of course, being a girl and beautiful and self-possessed; and she was as scornful of me as if she had been twenty-one, and a queen.

We went into the house by a side door — the great front entrance had two chains across it — and the first thing I noticed was that the passages were all dark. She picked up a lighted candle, and we went through more passages and up a huge staircase, until at last we came to a door.

"Go in," she said.

"After you, miss."

"Don't be ridiculous, boy. *I'm* not going in." And she walked away, taking the candle with her.

After a moment I knocked, and was told from within to enter. I went in and found myself in a large room, well lit with wax candles, but no glimpse of daylight could be seen. Everything in the room — furniture, curtains, scattered clothes — was old and musty.

On a chair by the dressing-table sat the strangest lady I have ever seen, or will ever see. She was dressed in rich materials — satins, and

lace, and silks — all of faded white. She had not quite finished dressing, and her bright jewels and trinkets lay on her table beside the looking-glass.

"Who is it?" said the lady.

"Pip, ma'am."

"Pip?"

"Mr Pumblechook's boy, ma'am. Come, to play."

"Come nearer. Let me look at you. Come closer."

It was when I stood before her that I could see that her face was white too, and saw all the objects around her in detail. I noticed that a clock in the room had also stopped at twenty minutes to nine.

"Look at me," said Miss Havisham. "You're not afraid of a woman who has never seen the sun since before you were born?"

"No," I lied.

"Do you know what I touch here," she said, laying her right hand on her left side.

"Your heart, ma'am?"

"Broken!"

She laid great emphasis on the word, and kept her hand there for some time. "Oh, I'm tired. I

want diversion, and I've done with men and women. Now play. Play!"

I cannot think of an order in the world more difficult to obey; indeed I felt almost incapable of any movement at all.

"Are you sullen and obstinate?"

"No, ma'am, but I can't just — play. If you complain of me I shall get into trouble with my sister, so I would do it if I could. But it's so new here, and so strange, and so sad —"

I stopped, fearing I might say too much, or for that matter, had done so already.

She turned her eyes from me, and took up her looking-glass, and gazed into it. "So new to him," she muttered, "so old to me; so strange to him, so familiar to me; and so sad to both of us. Call Estella."

As she was still looking at herself, I thought she was still talking to herself.

"Call Estella!" she repeated, flashing a hard look at me. "You can do that! Call Estella!"

To stand in the dark in a mysterious passage of an unknown house, bawling Estella to a scornful young lady, and feeling it a liberty to speak her name at all, was almost as bad as trying to play to order.

But she answered at last and stood before Miss Havisham, who was now sitting at a small table in the middle of the room.

"My dear, let me see you play cards with this boy."

"With *him*? But he is a common labouring-boy!"

I thought I heard Miss Havisham's answer as she leaned towards the girl, only it seemed so unlikely: "Well! You can break his heart!"

"What do you play, boy?" asked Estella, sitting down.

"Nothing but beggar my neighbour, miss."

"Beggar him, Estella," said Miss Havisham, and we sat down to play cards.

"He calls the knaves Jacks, this boy!" cried Estella before our first game was finished. "And what coarse hands he has!"

I had never thought of being ashamed of my hands before, but I was now. Her contempt for me was so strong that it became infectious, and I caught it.

She won the game, and I dealt. That is, I misdealt, and she denounced me for being a stupid, clumsy labouring-boy.

"You say nothing of her," remarked Miss Havisham to me as she looked on. "She says many hard things of you, yet you say nothing of her. What do you think of her?"

"I — I don't like to say."

"Tell me in my ear," said Miss Havisham, bending down and leaning towards me.

"I think she's very proud," I whispered.

"Anything else?"

"I think she's very pretty."

"Anything else?"

"I think she's very insulting."

"Anything else?"

"I think I should like to go home."

"And never see her again, though she is so pretty?"

"I should like to see her again, but I should like to go home now."

Miss Havisham straightened in her chair. "You shall go soon," she said aloud. "Play the game out."

place to hide my face, and slipped down to the brewery wall, and cried. And as I cried I kicked the wall, trying to get rid of my injured feelings. In a while I returned, and the food and the beer made me feel a little better.

After a quarter of an hour or so Estella came down, carrying the keys, and touched me with a taunting hand.

"Why don't you cry," she said.

"Because I don't want to."

"You do. You've been crying till you are half blind, and you are near crying again now."

She laughed, and unlocked the gate, and let me out. I went straight to Mr Pumblechook's, and was relieved to find him out. So, leaving word in his shop that I was wanted at Miss Havisham's the following Tuesday, I set off on the four-mile walk to the forge. I pondered as I went along on all that I had seen, and thought that I was much more common and ignorant than I had ever considered myself until that morning.

I played the game to an end with Estella, and she won again. Then she threw the cards down on the table, as if she despised them for being won off me.

"When shall I have you here again?" said Miss Havisham. "Let me think."

I was beginning to remind her that it was Wednesday when she checked me with an impatient movement of her right hand.

"I know nothing of days of the week; I know nothing of weeks of the year. Come again after six days. Do you hear?"

"Yes, ma'am."

"Estella, take him down. Let him have something to eat and drink, and he can roam about if he wants before he leaves. Now go, Pip."

I followed the candle down, as I had followed it up, and when I finally came into the daylight I felt as if I had been in that room for many hours.

Estella left me in the courtyard and returned a few minutes later with some bread and meat and a small mug of beer. She put it down on the ground, as though I were a dog in disgrace, and I was so hurt that tears started to my eyes. The moment they sprang there the girl looked at me with a delight in having been the cause of them. Then, with a contemptuous toss of the head, she left me.

When she was gone, I looked about me for a

When I reached home my sister was very curious to know all about Miss Havisham's, and I soon found myself being cuffed about because my

answers were not thought long enough. The worst of it was that Mr Pumblechook came over at tea-time to have the details given to him, and his manner and nosiness made me keep my answers even shorter.

When Mr Pumblechook asked me what Miss Havisham was like, and I replied 'tall, thin and dark', and he replied 'Good!', I realized that he had never set eyes on the lady, and I could not then stop myself playing games on them. I told them that Miss Havisham sat in a black velvet sedan-chair in her room, that we ate cake off gold plates and drank wine out of goblets, and that Estella and I played with flags and swords.

If they had asked any more questions I think I would have betrayed myself, but then Joe came in for his tea and my sister insisted on relating my tales to him. While she and Mr Pumblechook sat debating whether I would be rewarded with property or money or both as a result of my visits, Joe was sent back to the forge by his wife for daring to suggest that I may receive nothing at all.

After Mr Pumblechook had driven off, I stole into the forge to Joe, and remained by him until he had finished for the night.

"Before the fire goes out, Joe, I should like to tell you something."

"Should you, Pip? Then tell us."

"About Miss Havisham's, Joe — it isn't true."

"You don't mean to say it's lies, Pip?"

129

"Yes, all of it. Terrible, isn't it?"

"Terrible? That it is, Pip. What possessed you?"

"I don't know, Joe. I don't know. It just happened."

I told Joe that I was very miserable, that I hadn't been able to explain myself to Mrs Joe and Mr Pumblechook, that there had been a beautiful girl at Miss Havisham's who was so proud, and that she had said I was common, and that I knew I was common, and that the lies had come out of it somehow, but I didn't know how.

"There's one thing you can be sure of, Pip," said Joe after some thought. "Namely, that lies is lies. However they come, they didn't ought to come. Don't you tell no more of 'em, Pip. That ain't the way to get out of being common, old chap. As to being common, I can't make it out —

you're an uncommon scholar."

"I've learned next to nothing, Joe. You think a lot of me, that's all."

"Well, Pip, you must be a common scholar afore you can be an uncommon one. The king upon his throne can't write his acts of parliament without having begun by learning his alphabet, though I can't say I've exactly done it."

I was touched by Joe's words, and asked him if we was angry with me.

"No, Pip, I ain't. But bearing in mind what you've done, you'd better drop it into your prayers when you go upstairs to bed. That's all, old chap, and don't never do it no more!"

I did include it in my prayers, but I wasn't long in bed before I began thinking how common Estella would consider Joe, and how coarse his hands, and how crude his ways.

3 I Become an Apprentice

It struck me next morning that the best step I could take towards making myself more uncommon was to get out of Biddy everything she knew — and it happened that on Thursday, after delivering groceries to a neighbour, she would always collect me at my house on the way to her grandmother's class.

"Biddy," I said cautiously before we set out for the village, "I know that you're more learned than me . . ."

"Than *I*, Pip," she laughed. "Than *I*!"

"— that you're more learned than I. But, well, could you teach me?"

"Of course, Pip, whenever I can. But I'm not that much of a scholar."

She may not have been the most beautiful girl in the world, Biddy Worple, but she was certainly the most obliging. She began her instruction right then, on the walk to the village, and by the time I arrived at Miss Havisham's the following week I firmly believed I had made some considerable progress in the knowledge of things.

As before, Estella locked the gate after admitting me to Satis House, and led me across

the courtyard. When we reached the middle she suddenly stopped, and put her face quite close to mine: "Well?"

"Well, miss," I answered, almost bumping into her.

"Am I pretty?"

"Yes, I think you're very pretty."

"And am I insulting?"

"Not as much as you were last time."

"Not as much?"

"No."

She then kicked me on the shin as hard as she could, and I clutched my leg in pain.

"What do you think of me now, you coarse little monster?"

"I won't tell you."

"You're going to tell upstairs — is that it?"

"No, that's not it at all."

"Why don't you cry, you little wretch?"

"Because I'll never cry for you again," I said — which was, I suppose, as false a declaration as was ever made.

Just then I heard a deep voice behind me, from near the barred window.

"And whom have we here?"

The voice belonged to a large, burly man, whose great face was dominated by thick lips and a beak nose.

"A boy, Mr Jaggers," said Estella.

"A boy of the neighbourhood?"

"Yes, sir," I said.

"And how do you come to be here?"

"Miss Havisham sent for me, sir."

"Well, behave yourself. I have a pretty large experience of boys, and you're a bad set of fellows. So you mind out, and behave yourself."

With these words he disappeared, and I followed Estella on the route she had taken

before, until she left me with Miss Havisham.

"So, the days have worn away, have they?"

"Yes, ma'am. Today is —"

"I don't want to know! Are you ready to play?"

"I don't think I am, ma'am, I'm afraid."

"Since this house strikes you as old and grave, boy, and you are unwilling to play, perhaps you are willing to work?"

"Yes, ma'am."

"Then you may take me for a walk," she said, rising from her chair and offering me her arm. "Come on, walk me!"

I walked her round the room several times like an invalid, and then she gestured to me to open two tall doors. They led to a spacious, musty room, dominated by a long table laden with all kinds of dusty, cobweb-ridden things. Spiders, beetles and mice ran all over it, apparently unmoved by our entrance.

"This is where I shall be laid when I am dead," she said. "This is where they will come and look at me. What do you think that is, where those cobwebs are?"

"I can't guess what it is, ma'am."

"It's a great cake. A wedding cake. My wedding cake. Mine!"

She paused for a moment, staring at the appalling sight on the table.

"Today is my birthday, Pip, but I don't suffer it to be mentioned. On this day of the year, long before you were born, this heap of decay was brought here. It and I have worn away together. The mice have gnawed away at it, and sharper teeth than those of mice have gnawed away at me."

She suddenly looked tired, and sighed heavily. "When the ruin is complete, and when they lay me dead in my bride's dress on the bride's table, so much the better if it is done on this day of the year!"

She looked at the table as though in a dream, then turned to me. "Call Estella!"

We played cards as before, and I lost as before, and Estella treated me as before, though she did not speak. After half-a-dozen games, Miss Havisham said: "Estella, take Pip down for some lunch. I expect he would like to sit in the courtyard. Is there sun today?"

"Yes, ma'am," I replied. "It's a fine day."

"I'm sure it is. Now, Pip, you must come again in five days. Goodbye."

Estella left me sitting on a bench in the courtyard, and then returned with some lunch, once again putting it on the ground in front of me, before vanishing again. I was just about to eat when I was confronted by a pale, tall boy.

"Who let you in?" he asked.

"Miss Estella," I replied.

"I see. Let's go and fight!"

I have since often asked myself why I did what he said, but his manner was so final that I followed him as if under a spell. He led on a few paces, then took off his jacket.

"I ought to give you a reason for fighting, I suppose," he said, and then he butted my stomach with his head.

This both hurt and annoyed me, and I squared up to fight him. But I was quite frightened, for though of my own age he was taller than I and made a great show with his fists. "Laws of the game!" he declared, bobbing and weaving in front of me. "Regular rules!"

I have never been so surprised as when, after taking several weak punches from him, I let out the first real blow and saw him lying on his back, holding his cheek. He shaped up to me again, tapped me a few times, and then I knocked him

sometimes she would tell me that she hated me; sometimes she would be quite familiar with me. But never again did she tell me I might kiss her.

We had fun, now and then. Miss Havisham quite took to a blacksmith's working song I sang once, and we would often sing it as we walked; even Estella joined in once or twice.

The only person who knew of all this was Biddy, to whom I told everything. I could not bring myself to tell Joe of my fight, and after that found it difficult to relate the details of the happenings at the big house — let alone my new feelings.

Discussions went on endlessly between my sister and Mr Pumblechook as to the outcome of these visits, but Joe took little part in them. His wife took this to mean that, since I was now old enough to be apprenticed to Joe, he was not favourable to my being taken away from the forge.

Then, one morning, nearly a year after my first visit to Satis House, Miss Havisham asked me to take Joe with me the next time; and so, after leaving Mrs Joe at Mr Pumblechook's house, I led a very nervous blacksmith, dressed in his Sunday best, to the strange house.

"I understand that you are the husband of Pip's sister," began Miss Havisham, "and that the boy is to be apprenticed to you. Is that so, Mr Gargery?"

Joe was almost too terrified to reply. "Yes, ma'am, that is, I mean to say, yes, he is."

"And does the boy have any objection."

down again; and again; and again. Finally he stayed down, looking up at me through reddened eyes: "That means you've won!"

His spirit inspired me with great respect, and I felt no satisfaction in my victory.

"Can I help you?" I asked, offering my hand.

"No, thank you."

"Then — goodbye."

"The same to you."

When I reached the courtyard I found Estella with the keys, but instead of going towards the gate she stepped back near some bushes, and beckoned me to follow.

"Come here," she said. "You may kiss me if you like."

I kissed her cheek as she turned it to me. I would have gone through a good deal to kiss Estella — but I felt the kiss was given to the coarse boy as a piece of money might be given, and that it was worth nothing of any value.

On my next visit to Satis House I learned that I was expected to walk Miss Havisham round the two rooms she used for as much as three hours at a time. This I did on every visit I made there, which from now on was every other day.

We soon began to know each other a little better, and I told her of my desire to learn more. But she did not help me in this; indeed she seemed to prefer me to remain ignorant. I received nothing on all these occasions but my daily dinner.

Estella was always there, and always led me in and out. Sometimes she would coldly tolerate me; sometimes she would condescend to me;

"No, ma'am, not so far as I know. But if Pip had no heart for the life of a smithy, I wouldn't try to force my wishes on him."

"Well, Pip has been a good boy here and earned a premium. There are twenty-five guineas in this bag. Give it to your master, Pip."

Joe could hardly believe his ears and was almost speechless.

"Thank you, ma'am, thank you kindly. I — I don't know what to say."

"Am I to come again, Miss Havisham?" I asked.

"No, Gargery is your master now. Goodbye, Pip."

Estella spoke not a word as she led us out and locked the door behind us. Once outside, Joe leaned his back against the courtyard wall: "Astonishing, Pip. This is a-stonishing!" And he kept murmuring that, or something very like it, at intervals all the way back to Mr Pumblechook's house.

Once Mrs Joe and Mr Pumblechook had taken this news in, and the corn-chandler had wallowed in my sister's declarations of gratitude for introducing me to Miss Havisham, I was taken round to the town hall to have my indentures to J. Gargery signed by a magistrate. That evening, a little of the twenty-five guineas was spent on a dinner at the Blue Boar, but I could not bring myself to enjoy it, and felt like a commodity that had been bought at a sale.

At last, when I finally got to my little bedroom, I was truly wretched, and knew I should never like Joe's trade. I had liked the idea once, but once was not now. I had believed in the forge as the glowing road to manhood, but in a single year all that was changed. Now it seemed

coarse and common, and I saw a future of dull endurance set out for me. I knew my feelings were ungracious, even ungrateful, but I could not help them. I felt ashamed of my home and who I was.

Looking back now, I can see that I served my apprenticeship and never ran away not because I was faithful, but because Joe was faithful; and that I worked hard not because I saw virtue in it, but because Joe did. Any good that came from that apprenticeship came from Joe, and not from me.

Although I now no longer visited the school-room, I still had my special lessons from Biddy whenever I could; and, whenever I could, I tried to pass on my learning to Joe. One day, during one of these sessions, I suggested that I pay Miss Havisham a visit to thank her. Joe thought it a poor idea — he said Miss Havisham had been very final — but he nevertheless agreed to my taking a half-day holiday for the purpose.

My visit was short and far from sweet. A maid, not Estella, opened the gate, and Miss Havisham was quite sharp with me.

"Well, Pip," she said, "I hope you want nothing — for you'll get nothing."

"No, indeed, Miss Havisham. I only wanted you to know that I am doing well in my apprenticeship, and am always obliged to you."

"Come now and then, Pip. Yes, come on your birthday." She tapped her fingers on her dressing-table. "I see you're looking round for Estella. Well, she's abroad, educating for a lady, and far out of reach; prettier than ever and admired by all who see her. Do you feel you have lost her?"

There was unpleasant enjoyment in her voice, and she spared me the trouble of replying by curtly dismissing me; but the news of Estella had made me all the more dissatisfied with my lot.

On the way back through the town I met Joe, and we walked the four miles to the house together. Late in the afternoon we heard the gun of the prison-ship, warning of an escape, and my mind raced back to the encounters with my convict.

The house was quiet, and as we approached I had the sensation of something being wrong. We opened the door and there, on the kitchen floor, was Mrs Joe, her body lying in the strangest of positions. She was unconscious, knocked down, it seemed, by a severe blow to the back of her head.

The next few days are a blur to me — a confusion of doctors, constables and soldiers — as my sister lay helpless in bed, her speech gone, her hearing impaired, her memory damaged. She communicated her needs by feebly writing with chalk on a slate, but with her letters being so bad she was sometimes offered the wrong food and drink. We were at a loss to find suitable help for her until, following the death of Mr Worple's great aunt, Biddy came to look after her — and indeed to look after us.

Strangely, Mrs Joe was altogether a person of a different disposition now, patient and understanding, though every few weeks she would have a relapse and hold her head in her hands for hours on end, wailing dreadfully. It was during one of these bouts, some nine months after the attack, that my sister died.

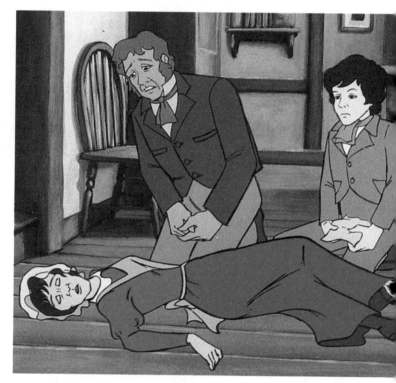

4 My Life is Changed

I now fell into a regular routine of apprentice life — a life which was varied only by the arrival of my birthday and another visit to Miss Havisham. The interview lasted but a few minutes, and she gave me a guinea; as I left she told me to come again on my next birthday, and this became an annual custom.

At home, Biddy was a very different housekeeper from Mrs Joe, and she found time to improve her learning a good deal. In the summer we used to go walking out on the marshes, and on one such occasion I told her of my feelings about my calling in life, and of my desire to be a gentleman. Biddy was, as usual, understanding and considerate — and she knew what had caused these feelings in me — but neither she nor I could see the remotest way I could even begin to bring about such a change in my fortunes.

Then, quite suddenly, in the third year of my apprenticeship to Joe, an event occurred which was indeed to change the course of my life.

Joe and I were working in the forge one bright morning when we had a visitor. He did not recognize me, but I certainly recognized him — as the man I had seen in the garden on my second visit to Satis House.

"Do I address Joe Gargery?" he began.

"You do," replied Joe, shutting off the bellows.

"And is this Pip, your apprentice?"

"It is. And could I ask your name, sir?"

"My name is Jaggers, and I am a lawyer in London — a pretty well-known lawyer. I have unusual business with you, and I will start by explaining that it is not of my creation. If my advice had been asked, I should not have been here. What I have to do as the confidential agent of another, I do; no less, no more."

Our visitor came up closer to us. "Now, Joseph Gargery, I am the bearer of an offer to relieve you of this young fellow. You would not object to cancel his indentures, at his request and for his good?"

"No, sir. Lord forbid that I should stand in Pip's way."

"Then the communication I have is that this young fellow has great expectations."

Joe and I gasped, and looked at one another.

"I am instructed to communicate to him," continued Mr Jaggers, talking to Joe but waving his fat finger sideways at me, "that he will come into a handsome property. Further, that it is the desire of the present owner of that property that he be immediately removed from this place and be brought up as a gentleman — in a word, as a young man of great expectations."

My dream was out; my wild fancy was sober reality: Miss Havisham was going to make my fortune on a grand scale.

"Now, Mr Pip, you are to understand, first, that it is the request of your benefactor that you will always bear the name 'Pip'. You are to understand, second, that the name of your benefactor remains a profound secret until that person chooses to reveal it, and that secret is held only by the person from whom you derive your expectations and myself. It is the intention of the person to reveal it at first hand to yourself, but where and when I cannot say; it may be years hence. You are to understand, third, that you are prohibited from making any mention or inquiry in this direction; if you have a suspicion in your breast as to the identity of your benefactor, you must keep it there. You will please consider me as your guardian. Now, do you object to any of these conditions?"

"No — no, sir," I stammered.

"I should think not. We come next to mere details of arrangement. You must know that although I use the term 'expectations' more than once, you are not endowed with expectations only. There is already in my possession a sum of money sufficient for your education and maintenance, and the way will be prepared for you. Now, when will you come to London? Shall we say a week from today?"

Mr Jaggers gave me twenty pounds to buy clothes and my ticket, as well as a card with his London address; but Joe, despite being pressed, refused to take any money for the loss of my services. The lawyer then left, leaving Joe and I stunned and speechless.

Both Joe and Biddy, though sad at the prospect of my going, were almost as pleased for me as I was for myself. The first chance that Biddy and I had to be alone, I suggested that she should help Joe in his learning and his manners, ready for the day when I was able to help him move on to a higher sphere of activity in life.

"Have you never considered that he may be proud?"

"Proud?" I replied.

"Yes. He may be too proud to let anyone take him out of a place he's competent to fill, and fills well and with respect. To tell the truth, I think he is, though you must know him far better than I do."

"I am very sorry to see this in you, Biddy. I did not expect it. You are envious, Biddy, and grudging. You are dissatisfied on account of my rise in fortune, and you can't help showing it."

"Whether you scold me or approve of me, Pip, you may depend on my trying to do all that lies in my power, here, at all times. And whatever opinion you take away of me, it shall make no difference to my remembrance of you. Yet a gentleman should not be unjust."

When I went into the town to buy my new clothes a few days later I called on Mr Pumblechook, and he could not have been more obliging. He congratulated both of us in equal measure for my good fortune, and wined and dined me as though I were already a man of fortune.

I then made my way to see Miss Havisham.

"Well, Pip," she said curtly, "and what brings you here away from your birthday?"

"I start for London tomorrow, Miss Havisham," I replied, choosing my words with care, "and I thought you would not mind my taking leave of you. I have come into much good fortune since I saw you last, and I am very grateful for it."

"Yes, yes, I have seen Mr Jaggers. I have

heard about it. So you are adopted by a rich person, not named, and Mr Jaggers is your guardian?"

"Yes, Miss Havisham."

"Well, you have a promising career before you. Be good — deserve it — and abide by Mr Jaggers' instructions. Goodbye, Pip."

She stretched out her hand, and I put it to my lips; and then I left my fairy godmother.

The coach was to stop at six o'clock the next morning on its way to London. The parting from Biddy and Joe was sad and tearful, but soon I could think of nothing but the exciting times that lay before me.

I was frightened at first by the great size of London, but I was also disappointed, for it was for the most part ugly, crooked, narrow and dirty. Mr Jaggers' office was near Smithfield, and there he told me of the arrangements that had been made on my behalf. I was to go to the rooms of one Herbert Pocket, son of Mr Matthew Pocket — whose name I had heard mentioned in conversations between Miss Havisham and Estella, and who was now to be my tutor.

The house I was to occupy off Chancery Lane was hardly what I had expected for a person of

my new standing, and I felt a sense of being cheated as I climbed the broken staircase to a dark landing and the door marked *Mr Pocket, Junior*. My concern about the surroundings vanished when the tenant opened the door to greet me — for Mr Pocket, Junior turned out to be none other than the pale young gentleman I had fought with in the gardens of Satis House!

"The idea of it being *you*," he said.

"And the idea of it being *you*," I replied.

"I do hope you will forgive me for knocking you about so dreadfully."

At this we both burst out laughing, and he invited me inside. He showed me around the rooms, and when we had a cup of tea I asked Herbert what he had been doing at Miss Havisham's house that day.

"Miss Havisham had sent for me," he began, "to see if she could take a fancy to me. But she couldn't — or rather, she didn't. If I had come out of it successfully, I suppose I should I have been provided for. Perhaps I should have been engaged to Estella."

"How did you bear such disappointment."

"I didn't care much for the idea, Pip. That girl's hard and haughty and capricious, and has been brought up by Miss Havisham to wreak revenge on all the male sex."

"Why?" I asked. "What revenge?"

"Lord, Pip! Don't you know? Well, it's quite a story — and it shall be saved until dinner."

Meantime, Herbert explained that he had been asked by his father, on behalf of Mr Jaggers, to take me in on my arrival in London; and that if things worked out well, this arrangement could become permanent. He said that my guardian was Miss Havisham's man of business and solicitor, and ran all her affairs.

Herbert Pocket had a frank and easy way with him that was very engaging, and I soon felt him to be a friend. He was amiable and cheerful, yet his figure was a little ungainly, and he was still very much the pale young gentleman.

I was burning with curiosity about the story of Miss Havisham when we sat down to dinner — a meal furnished entirely from the local coffee-house — but before he could start Herbert was forced to point out that it was not the custom for

young gentlemen to put their knife in their mouth — as I was about to do. Indeed it is worth noting here that throughout this meal — and throughout the first months of our subsequent times together — he constantly educated me in the correct ways of all kinds of social manners; and that he did so in such a friendly and endearing fashion that neither of us ever felt even slightly embarrassed by the process.

"Now," he said, taking a deep breath, "Miss Havisham was a spoilt child, as you must know. Her mother died when she was young, and her father denied her nothing. Her father was a country gentleman, and a brewer, down in your part of the country. He was very rich and very proud — and so was his daughter.

"When he died, Miss Havisham was in her youth, and she now became an heiress. She was seen as a great match, and attracted many proposals of marriage. Now, there appeared on the scene — at the races, at the balls, at the parties, anywhere you like — a certain man, who courted Miss Havisham and made love to her. He professed to be devoted to her, and there is no doubt that she perfectly idolized him. The wedding was arranged, and the great day came. But not the bridegroom. He wrote a letter —"

"Which she received when she was dressing for her marriage?" I interrupted. "At twenty minutes to nine?"

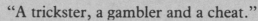

"A trickster, a gambler and a cheat."

"So why didn't he marry her and come into all the property?"

"I don't know, Pip. He had got his hands on a good deal of her money before that day, and perhaps he was married already."

"Do you know what happened to him?"

Herbert shrugged his shoulders. "Not exactly. I believe he fell into deeper shame and ruin, and there were stories that he had gone to prison."

"And Estella was adopted?"

"Yes, and brought up to hate men. There has always been an Estella, ever since I have heard of Miss Havisham, but I know no more. Now, there is a perfectly open understanding between us. All I know about Miss Havisham, you know."

"And all I know," I replied, "you know."

"Good. So there can be no competition between us. As to the condition that you may not inquire or discuss the identity of your benefactor — you may be very sure that it will be never be touched upon, or even approached, by me or anyone belonging to me."

And so, for the present, the subject of Miss Havisham and Estella was closed.

"The very hour and minute," continued Herbert, nodding, "at which she stopped all the clocks in the place. When she recovered from a bad illness she laid the whole place waste, as you have seen it, and she has never since looked upon the light of day."

"Who was this man who broke her heart?"

Herbert worked in the City of London, at a company insuring ships and their cargoes. But he was quick to tell me of his plans to one day be a shipper of all kinds of exotic goods himself. There came on me, however, the strong impression that Mr Pocket, Junior would never be rich and successful, and that he would always endure his own strange kind of well-to-do poverty.

The two of us got along famously, and over the next few days he introduced me to the life of London: to the theatre, to the drinking clubs, to the restaurants, to the great buildings, to the royal parks, and to the river — with which I fell so much in love that I later bought a rowing boat. And all the time, I learned from him the essentials of being a gentleman.

On the first Sunday we went to visit his family's home in Hammersmith — a large family of seven children, living in a large house with two young gentleman lodgers — and Mr Pocket, Senior informed me he had been asked to be my tutor. No particular training or occupation was intended: simply an accumulation of knowledge on all relevant things. Thus while Herbert Pocket was to improve my manners, his father was to improve my mind, and a weekly schedule was arranged for this purpose.

The following Monday I went to see Mr Jaggers to tell him of these arrangements, and discovered that I had only to ask for money and it would be provided there and then by his clerk. As a result I soon contracted expensive habits, and began to spend an amount of money that a few short months before I should have thought almost fabulous. Thus began my life of a young gentleman in London.

5 Returns from Abroad

Several months of this carefree existence had passed when I received a letter from Biddy, informing me that Joe was to visit me the following day on a matter of importance. I was filled with dread, for I was already part of a different world, and the distance between Joe's marshlands and the crowded streets of London seemed almost too great to bridge.

Unfortunately Herbert was at home when he arrived in his Sunday best, and I found Joe's crude ways and humble manners — he called me 'sir' — irritating and embarrassing. He had, it appeared, been approached by his uncle Mr Pumblechook on behalf of Miss Havisham; she wished me to visit Satis House and see Estella, who had returned from France. Quite why the message had come this strange route I never did discover — Miss Havisham could have written to Mr Jaggers, or Biddy could have conveyed the message in her letter — but in any case I was only too delighted with the invitation, and set out the next day for Satis House.

In the coach I pondered the reason for this journey, and on Miss Havisham's plans for me. She had adopted Estella, and she had as good as adopted me, and it could not fail to be her intention to bring us together. It must be for me to restore the desolate house, admit the sunlight into the dark rooms and set the clocks going — to do all the shining deeds of the young knight of romance, and marry the princess.

I was let in at the gate by a servant I had not seen before, and found my way to Miss Havisham's door.

"Pip's rap," I heard her say. "Come in, Pip!"

She was sitting in front of the dressing-table, as unchanged as ever. "Well?"

"I heard, Miss Havisham, that you were so kind as to wish me to come and see you, and I came directly."

"Well, you are quite the young gentleman now, Pip. You have obviously made good use of your fortune."

I was about to reply when the door opened and in walked a captivating young woman. It was Estella, as distant and divine as ever.

"Do you find her much changed, Pip?" asked Miss Havisham, with her greedy look.

"At first I did. But now I can see the old Estella, and it's a beautiful sight to behold."

"What! Come now, Pip, you found the old Estella proud and insulting. Don't you remember?"

"Yes, Miss Havisham, but —"

"Is *he* changed, my dear?" she cut in, talking to Estella.

"Very much," said Estella, looking at me.

"Less coarse and common?" inquired Miss Havisham, laughing.

Estella nodded, and laughed too. She treated me as a boy still, but lured me on.

"You've both changed, which is as it should be. But I have not. Nothing has changed here. Now, Estella, I would like a word with Pip."

As soon as Estella had left us, Miss Havisham turned on me. "Is she beautiful, graceful, well-grown? Do you admire her?"

"Everybody must who sees her, Miss Havisham."

"Love her, Pip, love her!" she whispered, grabbing my hand. "If she favours you, love her! If she wounds you, love her! If she tears your heart to pieces — and as it gets older and stronger it will tear deeper — love her, love her, *love her*!"

Never had I seen such passionate eagerness as was joined to the utterance of these words, yet she then suddenly let go of me and resumed her usual poise. "Estella is going to live with friends of mine in Richmond for a time, Pip, and I want you to accompany her there on the coach tomorrow, and see to it that no harm comes to her."

I said I would be only too happy to do so, and, no more being said on the subject, I took my leave. I stayed at the Blue Boar Inn in the town, excusing myself from visiting Joe and Biddy on the grounds of limited time.

On the coach the next morning, Estella and I talked of her schooling in France and my life in London and my friendship with Herbert, but

then I reminded her of our childhood — of her games, her taunts, and her kiss. She was proud and haughty still, but even more lovely, and I said so.

"Pip," she said, with a cold, careless smile, "will you never take warning?"

"Of what?"

"Of me."

"Warning not to be attracted by you, do you mean?"

"You silly boy. How can you talk such nonsense? You must know that I have no heart; no feelings, no sentiment. If you don't know what I mean, you are blind. I have not bestowed my affections elsewhere for I have none to bestow. And if we are to be thrown much together, you had better believe it at once."

I could and would not believe it. I loved her, adored her. But though she was now to live in Richmond, less than half-a-day's journey from my rooms, she may as well have been a thousand miles away.

Herbert seemed not in the least surprised when I told him of my feelings for Estella, and said that he had always known it; but he did, in the gentlest way, suggest that I abandon the cause, for she had all the faults of Miss Havisham. I would have none of it, and never gave up hope of winning her love.

I visited Estella several times in Richmond, but I always left with the peculiar impression that although I thought I would be happy with her, I was never happy when I *was* with her. She showed no signs of melting towards me — or towards any other as far as I could see, though she was greatly admired by many — and she still teased me mercilessly at times.

I soon settled back into my old life in London which, though for the most part enjoyable, was punctuated with bouts of boredom. The influences of my expectations in me were, I was aware, not all good; nor were they all beneficial to Herbert, since my lavish habits led his easy nature into expenses he could not afford.

We spent as much money as we could, but we were always more or less miserable, as most of our acquaintances were. There was a fiction among us that we were constantly enjoying ourselves, and a dark truth that we never really did.

I was always uneasy, too, about my behaviour towards Joe and Biddy. Sometimes I thought I should have been happier had I never seen Miss Havisham's face, and risen to manhood content to be partners with Joe in the old forge. But the longer I left it, the more difficult it became to do anything about it.

It was while I was in this melancholy frame of mind that I reached my twenty-first birthday — some eight months after Herbert had come of age — and I was asked by Mr Jaggers to visit his office. My guardian informed me, in disapproving tones, that he knew I was in debt, and handed me a note for five hundred pounds.

"Now that handsome sum of money is your own, in earnest of your expectations," he explained. "And you are to live at that rate, drawing one hundred and twenty-five pounds a quarter from my clerk, until your benefactor is revealed. As I have told you before, I am the mere agent. I execute my instructions, and am paid for doing so. I think them unwise, but I am not paid for giving any opinion on their merits."

Unknown to Mr Jaggers, I arranged through devious means over the next few weeks for money brokers to put one half of my gift Herbert's way, but the whole business was so cleverly managed that he had not the least suspicion that my hand was in it.

Some five or six months after my coming of age I returned to my rooms one wet night from dinner at a friend's house. Herbert was away in France on business for his firm and I climbed the stairs slowly, for I was not in a gay mood.

As I lowered my candle to put the key in the door, there was a sudden sound behind me, and then a voice.

"Mr Pip?"

I turned to see a large figure in the shadows on the landing, and I moved my lamp towards its face. I could see it was a man about sixty, hardened by exposure to the weather, and with a sinister patch over one eye.

"That is my name," I replied. "What is your business?"

"My business? Ah, yes, I will explain my business, by your leave."

"Do you wish to come in?"

"Yes, but there's no-one near, is there? No-one came with you, nor no-one inside?"

"Why do you, a stranger coming to my rooms at night, ask such a question?"

"Oh, you're a game one, that's for sure. I'm glad you've growed up a game one!"

Then I knew him! I could not recall a single feature, but I knew him! If the wind and the rain had driven away the intervening years, and swept us to the churchyard where we stood face to face, I could not have known my convict more distinctly than I knew him now.

"I think you had better come in." I said it calmly, though I was confused and shaken.

Once inside, and with the lamps lit, he took my hands, raised them to his lips, and kissed them. "You acted noble, my boy! Noble, Pip. And I've never forgot it!"

"If you have come here to thank me, it was not necessary," I said, taking away my hands. "Still, however you have found me out, there must be something good in the feeling that has brought you here. I am glad you have repented and recovered yourself, and I am glad you have come to thank me. But you must understand that I cannot wish to renew that chance intercourse with you of long ago, under these different circumstances."

He said nothing, but gazed at me with a slight smile.

"You are wet, and look weary. Will you drink something before you go."

He nodded, and I made him some hot rum and water. When he put it to his lips, I saw with amazement that he was weeping.

"I hope you do not think I spoke harshly to you just now. I had no intention of doing it, and I am sorry for it if I did. I wish you well, and happy."

He stretched out his hand to me, and I gave

him mine. Then I beckoned him to sit down.

"How are you living?" I asked.

"I've been a sheep-farmer, stock-breeder and other trades besides, many a thousand mile of stormy water from this."

"I hope you have done well."

"I've done wonderful well, Pip. I'm famous for it. But may I make so bold as to ask you how come you have done so well, since you and me was out on them shivering marshes?"

I told him, briefly, the story of how I had been chosen to succeed to some property.

At this point my visitor began asking a long series of leading questions about my life, though none required an answer and none was given. He knew every detail of my arrangements, to the last letter and penny, and the truth of my position gradually came upon me. I could not have spoken one word then, though it had been to save my life.

"Yes, Pip, dear boy, I've made a gentleman of you! It's *me* what has done it! I swore that time, sure as ever I earned a guinea, that guinea would go to you. I lived rough so that you should live smooth. I worked hard so that you should be above work. That hunted dog what you kept alive got his head so high that he could make a gentleman — and Pip, you're him!"

The dread I had of this man, and the distaste I felt for him, could not have been exceeded if he had been some terrible beast.

"Look'ee here, Pip. I'm your second father.

You're my son — more to me than any son. I've put away money, only for you to spend. When I was a hired-out shepherd in a lonely hut, not seeing no faces but faces of sheep till I half forgot what men's and women's faces was like, I see *your* face. And each time I says to myself, 'If I get liberty and money, I'll make that boy a gentleman.' And I done it!"

Again he took my hand and shook it, while my blood ran cold within me.

"Don't mind me talking, Pip, for you ain't looked slowly forward to this as I have. You wasn't prepared for this, as I was, I know that. But didn't you never think it might be me?"

"No, no," I replied. "Never!"

"Well, it was me, and single-handed. Not a soul in it but me and Mr Jaggers."

Oh, if that man had never come; if only he had left me at the forge — far from contented, yet by comparison so happy.

He took another great gulp of his drink. "When I was rich, I says to myself, 'If I ain't a gentleman, and got no learning, I'm the owner of such.' That's the way I kept myself going. I knew I would come for certain one day, and make myself known to you, on your own ground."

I tried to collect my thoughts, but I was still stunned.

"Where will you put me, dear boy? I must be put somewheres."

"You mean — to sleep?"

"Yes, and to sleep long and sound, for I've been tossed and washed by the sea for months."

"My friend is absent. You must — you must have his room."

Suddenly he stood over me, pointing his finger at my face. "Look'ee here, Pip. Caution is necessary."

"How do you mean — caution?"

"I was sent to Australia for life. I'm a free man there, for I won my pardon, but it's death to come back. I should be hanged for certain if I was took in England."

Nothing was needed but this. The wretched man, after loading me with his gold and silver for years, had risked his life to come to me, and I held it there, in my keeping. I explained that Herbert was not expected back for two more days, and that we would consider the best plan to follow in the morning.

When he had finally gone to bed — a pistol laying beside him on his pillow — I sat for hours in the drawing-room, trying to sort all this out in my swirling mind.

My first thoughts were of my ficticious benefactor. Miss Havisham's intentions towards me were all a mere dream! Estella was not designed for me; I was suffered at Satis House only as a convenience, a model to practise on when no other model was at hand.

But this was not the sharpest pain. That came when I realized that it was for a convict, a man whose crimes I did not know but who could be now taken from my rooms and hanged, that I had deserted Joe. I would not have gone back to Joe now, nor Biddy, for any consideration, because of my own worthless conduct. And I could never, never undo what I had done.

6 Fire and Water

My first concern the next morning was to invent an identity for my unwelcome guest, and as he devoured breakfast I explained that I would say he was my uncle. His name, it turned out, was Abel Magwitch, but on the prison-ship he had taken the name Provis, and we decided to stay with that. I also resolved to keep him in my rooms until Herbert returned and lodgings could be arranged.

That first afternoon I went to see Mr Jaggers, who of course knew of my visitor. He said he had counselled Magwitch against returning to England when he had written asking for my address, but he had been determined to come. Jaggers knew, too, that I had always believed Miss Havisham to be my benefactor, but he claimed, with ample justification, that he had never said nor done anything to encourage me in that mistaken belief.

The two days until Herbert's return seemed an age, particularly since we could go out only late at night and I was thus imprisoned with Provis for hour after hour. Dear Herbert was sworn to secrecy before being told the mysterious tale, and he obviously shared both my shock and my distaste for our visitor. His advice was to not forsake him, since he might become desperate and dangerous, but to work towards the goal of smuggling him out of the country.

That evening, having secured suitably discreet lodgings for Provis nearby in Essex Street, we asked him about his life — and especially with reference to the man on the marshes that cold Christmas Day. It was a long, sad story of struggle and cruelty and imprisonment, and I shall relate here only the chapter that touches directly on this other party.

"A matter of over twenty year ago," he began, taking a gulp of rum, "I got acquainted with a man whose skull I'd crack open now if ever I saw him. His right name was Compeyson, and that's the man, dear Pip, you saw me pounding in the ditch. He set up to be a gentleman, this Compeyson, and he had learning. He was a smooth one to talk to, and a dab hand at the ways of gentlefolks. He was good looking, too, and had a way with the women, though he were married.

" 'To judge from appearances, you're out of luck,' he says to me. 'Perhaps yours is going to change.' Well, Compeyson took me on to be his man and partner. But his business turns out to be swindling, forging, passing stolen money and such like. That man got me into such straits as

made me his black slave. I was always in debt to him, always under his thumb, always in danger for him. He'd no more heart than a lump of iron. He was as cold as death.

"At last he tried his tricks once too often, passing a forged note to a jeweller, and he was 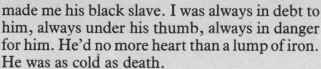 arrested in the street. And I was arrested after he told them where I was. At the trial he used his charms and educated ways on the judge, and blamed me for his troubles. And when we're sentenced, he gets seven years and I gets fourteen. I vowed then I'd do him for what he'd done to me.

"So on the prison-ship I got him a good one. I only gave him a scar, before they pulled me off, but I would have killed him if I could. Then I escaped — and he escaped too — and you saw, Pip, how I nearly killed him.

"Of course he had much the best of it to the last — his character was so good. He had escaped when he was made half wild by me and by my murderous intentions, and his punishment was light. But I was put in irons, brought to trial again and sent for life. But I didn't stay for life, for I won my pardon fair and square."

He wiped his brow with his handkerchief, and took another drink.

"Is he dead?" I asked.

"He hopes *I* am, if he's alive, you can be sure of that. I never heard no more of him."

Herbert was now writing with his pencil in the cover of a book. He pushed it over to me, as Provis gazed into the fire. I read: *Compeyson is the man who professed to be Miss Havisham's lover.*

I shut the book and nodded slightly to my friend, and put the book aside. We said nothing, but both looked at Provis as he stood smoking by the fire.

Neither Herbert nor I doubted the consequences if Compeyson were alive and should discover our secret. But we resolved not to mention anything about our plans for Provis — he seemed quite set on staying in England, despite the dangers — until I had made an important visit.

There was an air of utter loneliness at Satis House now, and though everything inside was unchanged, Miss Havisham seemed even more desolate than before.

"And what wind blows you here, Pip?" she inquired as I entered her morbid room.

"I have found out who my patron is, Miss Havisham. It is not a fortunate discovery, and is not likely to enrich me in reputation or fortune. There are reasons why I must say no more of that. It is not my secret, but another's."

"Well?"

"When you brought me here as a boy it was to torture me with Estella, wasn't it?"

"No, no, I —"

"And when I fell into the mistake I have so long remained in, you led me on."

"I *let* you *go* on, Pip. But you made your own snares. *I* never made them for you."

I knew it to be true. She was right about my folly, just as Jaggers had been right. I had

deluded myself, and it was senseless to blame others.

"Oh, Miss Havisham, there have been sore mistakes. My life has been a blind and thankless one. I want forgiveness and direction far too much to be bitter with you."

She turned her face to me for the first time since I had come in, and took both my hands in hers, and drew me to her, and began sobbing. "What have I done!" she cried. "What have I done!"

"If you mean what have you done to injure me, then the answer is very little. I should have loved Estella under any circumstances."

"I know, Pip, I know that. And now she is married to a cruel man."

I had been aware for some time that Estella was engaged, but these words still came as a shock, and served only to increase my misery — and hers.

"What have I done!" she repeated. "O, Pip, what have I done!" She wrung her hands, and clutched her head, and returned to this cry over and over again.

There was nothing more to be said. I left her, weeping, standing now by the fire, and made my way slowly downstairs. I had just reached the light of the courtyard when I heard a piercing scream from her room, and then another, longer one. I dashed back up the dark stairs, flung open the door and saw her running towards me, shrieking, a whirl of blazing flame all about her.

I snatched off my coat and smothered her with it, throwing her to the floor and dousing the flames on her writhing body. Then I grabbed the great cloth from the table, and with it dragged down the heap of ugly things that lay on it. We were on the floor struggling like desperate enemies, and it seemed that the closer I covered her, the more wildly she shrieked and tried to free herself. At last, as the black shower of her burnt dress fell around us, she lay still.

Assistance was sent for, and it was pronounced that her injuries, though serious, were far from hopeless; the main danger lay in the nervous shock. I stayed with her until the next day, until all worry was past (and to have my own singed hands dressed); then I attended to all the necessary details of such circumstances, including a letter to Estella. As I could then be of no further service, and had pressing reasons for leaving, I set out for London.

It became apparent soon after my return that Provis' presence in London was hardly a secret. Indeed from a network of sources — notably Mr Jaggers' clerk, with whom I had always been on excellent terms and who now reported on the news travelling around Newgate Prison — it was concluded not only that our movements were being closely watched, but that it was almost certain that the spy was none other than Compeyson.

We decided that Provis should lie low in a house down by the river at Limehouse, one belonging to the father of Herbert's fiancé, Clara. While well off my usual beat, Herbert was a frequent visitor and would act as messenger. The house was also well placed to slip our man on board a packet ship on the river.

Provis, who occupied the two cabin rooms at the top of the house, took all this in his stride and was reasonable throughout, though I stopped

short of informing him that the menace was Compeyson. His return was a venture, he said, and he had always known it to be a risky one. He would do nothing to make it more dangerous, and had little fear of his safety with such good help.

Herbert suggested that I move my boat from Hammersmith down to Blackfriars, and that we should be seen rowing regularly so that suspicions would not be aroused when the day came. Both Provis and I liked this scheme, and with everything arranged I rose to go, taking half an hour's start of Herbert.

"I don't like to leave you here," I said to Provis, "though I cannot doubt you are safer here than near me. Goodbye."

"Dear Pip," he said, clasping my hands. "I don't know when we will meet again, and I don't like goodbye. Say 'goodnight'."

"Goodnight. When the time comes you may be certain I shall be ready. Goodnight!"

The man's dignity in the circumstances, and his great trust in us, caused a change in my opinion of him, and over the next weeks I found, through Herbert, that he was, without losing my pity, gaining my respect.

We set to work the next week, though my hands were still a little painful. Sometimes I would go out alone, sometimes with Herbert;

and gradually the distance was extended, first past London Bridge and then, after some weeks, all the way down to the estuary at Erith. Though we heard no more information to alarm us, I could not get rid of the notion of being watched. Once felt, it is a haunting idea, and impossible to shake off.

My worldly affairs were now rather gloomy, and I was pressed for money by more than one creditor. Even I began to know the want of ready money in my pocket, but I had determined that

it would be a heartless fraud to take any more money from my benefactor.

After months of waiting and preparation, the day for our deed was finally set. Herbert had discovered two likely ships, the first leaving for Hamburg at six o'clock, the second bound for Antwerp at a quarter past that hour. If we failed to hail the first, there was always another chance of success with the second.

It was a cool but not unpleasant March night as Herbert and I set out from Blackfriars, I rowing and Herbert steering. Quietly we made our way to downstream to the Mill Pond Steps at Limehouse and there, as arranged, stood our cargo. We touched the jetty for a moment and he was aboard.

"Dear boy," he said, putting his hand on my shoulder as he took his seat. "Well done! Thank'ee."

Soon we were among the ships and the barges and the buoys, and we rowed within feet of both our vessels for a close look. Our plan was to run with the tide down to the long reaches below Gravesend, between Kent and Essex, where the estuary is broad and solitary, and choose a suitable resting-place until the arrival of the ships we intended to board.

The plan worked, but the two hours until the Hamburg boat came into view seemed like two days. We rowed quickly towards its channel, and then I stood up, waving my arms and shouting, "Passenger! Passenger!" for all I was worth. It was almost upon us before the paddles stopped churning, and it slowed to a halt.

Provis stood up and I took his hand. I told him how grieved I was that he should have risked so much for my sake.

"Dear boy, I've been content to take my chances. I've seen my boy — and he can be a gentleman now, with or without my help. Goodbye, Pip."

"Goodbye, and good luck."

There was no time for more, for the crew on the Hamburg ship threw down a ladder and a rope. Provis quickly shook hands with Herbert and thanked him heartily. Then one of the crew pointed to the bank, and shouted something to us in a language we did not understand. We all looked round — and there, heading towards us at a furious rate, was a Customs galley with uniformed officers and a passenger.

The sergeant at its bow shouted at us as he approached: "You have a returned transport there! His name is Abel Magwitch, otherwise Provis! I call on that man to surrender, and on you to assist!"

By now the Customs boat was almost on us, and there was no escape. Our cause was helpless. The sergeant continued to shout to us, and to the crew of the ship, when suddenly I recognized the man cringing in his galley.

Provis recognized him, too, and in a moment he was turned again into the beast I had encountered in the churchyard on the marshes.

"Compeyson!"

He dived headlong at the informer, and both

men crashed into the water. For a minute, maybe more, we could make out nothing; but then, some way off, Provis broke the surface, gasping for air. He swam, slowly, to the Customs galley, and they dragged him on board. Breathing fast and heavy, he collapsed in the bottom of the boat, clutching his side.

I knelt over him, from our boat, and he turned his head towards me. "I   I got 'im, young Pip," he said in a whisper. "At last — I got 'im!"

They put irons round my convict's legs, and rowed him to prison. I was allowed to go with him, for he was badly hurt, and as I sat there by his side, I felt that this was my rightful place while he still lived. My repugnance to him had all melted away, and I saw now only a man who had meant to be my benefactor, and who had felt affectionately, gratefully and generously towards me over many years.

He lay in the prison hospital very ill for the three weeks until the trial. He had broken two ribs, which had punctured a lung, and his breathing grew worse with every day.

The trial was short and clear, for nothing could deny the fact that he had returned to England, and it was impossible to do otherwise than find him guilty. He was one of thirty-two wretched men and women to be sentenced that dull April day, but in view of his exploits the judge paid special attention to him as he sat motionless in the crowded dock. The appointed punishment was death, and he was told he must prepare himself to die.

I earnestly hoped and prayed that he may die before the day of the hanging, but in the dread of his lingering on I wrote petitions to the Home Secretary and others in authority, setting forth my knowledge of him and explaining how it was that he had come back for my sake.

On the tenth day after the trial, and on my tenth visit, I found him in more discomfort than ever before, and his face was placid and ghostly.

"Are you in much pain today?"

"I don't complain of none, dear boy."

"You never do complain."

"Thank'ee, Pip, thank'ee. God bless you. You've never deserted me. God bless you — always."

He had spoken his last words. He smiled, and raised my hand to his lips. Then he gently let it sink again, with his own hands lying on it. The placid look came back, and passed away, and his head dropped on his still breast.

Epilogue

Within days of my convict's death I fell ill, and with Herbert married and gone to live in Egypt, I was very much alone. This illness soon developed into a delirious fever, and I imagined on several occasions that I saw Joe's face in my ravings. It was not until I was stable again, some weeks later, that I realized it *was* Joe — dear, kind, forgiving Joe. I was a child again in his care, and he nursed me back to health.

One morning, I woke to find him gone. He had left a simple note — Biddy had taught him to read and write! — and enclosed was a receipt for my debts. Until then I had always supposed that my creditors had suspended their proceedings because of my illness; but the receipt was in Joe's name, and the blacksmith had paid my debts in full.

I determined to follow Joe to the forge, to thank him. But that wasn't my main purpose: that was to see dear Biddy, and ask her to go through life with me. So, three days later, I set off for the marsh country once again.

I put up at the Blue Boar, but my stay was blighted by the presence at dinner of Mr Pumblechook. He laid into me about my ingratitude — I had not been to visit his nephew nor him once all these years — and about fate now dealing me the blows I merited.

I was still pondering his outburst when I arrived at the forge. There I found Biddy, and Joe; they were arm in arm at the door of the house, as two youngsters who were in love. And indeed they were — and to be married the very next week.

I have often thought since how thankful we should all be that I had never breathed a word of my last pathetic hope to Joe. They deserved each other, and were so happy; and I was so pleased for both their sakes, if not for mine.

I sold all I had, and put aside as much as I could, and went out to join Herbert. When the matter of Egypt had first come up, shortly after the capture of my 'uncle', Herbert and Clara had entreated me to go to them, for a trial period if necessary, since he could offer me the position of clerk.

Many a year went round before I gained an interest in the business, but I lived happily with the Pockets, and maintained a constant correspondence with Joe and Biddy. We were not in a grand way of business, but we had a good name, and worked hard for our profits.

I had not seen Joe nor Biddy for eleven years when, one evening in October, I laid my hand on the latch of the old kitchen door — so softly that I was not heard, and I looked in unseen. There, smoking his pipe in the old place by the firelight, sat Joe; and there, fenced into the corner with Joe's leg, and sitting on my own stool looking at the fire, was — me!

Joe explained they had given him the name of Pip for my sake, and had hoped he might grow a little bit like me — and thought he had. I thought he had, too, and was flattered. I took the boy out for a walk the next morning, up to the churchyard, and when I perched him on a certain tombstone, he showed me which grave was sacred to the memory of Philip Pirrip, late of this parish.

When Biddy gently brought up the subject of Estella, I knew I should have to go up to Satis House one last time. Joe had told me when he had been my nurse that Miss Havisham was dead, and that Estella had received most of the estate, and shortly afterwards the house had been put up for auction.

I had heard since of Estella as leading an unhappy life, soon separated from her cruel and mean husband. I had heard of his death, too, from a riding accident, but for two years, I had heard nothing more.

There was no house now, and no brewery — just the old walled garden, overgrown and desolate. I had been in the courtyard only moments when I glimpsed a woman, and she saw me. It was Estella.

We talked of our melancholy past, and a new bond sprang up between us. I took her hand in mine, and we left the ruined place; and, just as the morning mists had risen long ago when I first left the forge, so the evening mists were rising now, and in all the broad expanse of tranquil light they showed to me, I saw no shadow of another parting from her.